CAT AND MOUSE

"Know a girl by the name of Myra Campbell?"

The sudden question caused Patrick to blink. Then he carefully considered the tip of his cigarette, and then shook his head. "Myra Campbell? Can't say I do. Blonde, brunette, or redhead?"

Inspector Hood didn't answer; his eyes were wandering round the cramped flat. "She's Mrs. Hull's personal maid," he said.

"Never heard of her, anyway," Patrick said. "The villains make a nice haul?"

"Somewhere in the region of forty thousand pounds."

Ted Patrick whistled quietly through his teeth. He took another gulp from his glass. He looked sympathetically at the stolid figure in the chair. "Wish I could help, but I've never known anyone as ambitious as that. What about the car? If it ran down the copper, there should be marks on it."

"We're looking. We think it was ditched somewhere in the vicinity. It'll be found." He sounded confident enough.

"I hope it gives you a lead," Patrick said quietly. "When you find it." And then with a wistful smile: "And so save innocent people who happen to be unlucky enough to have their names on your books having their pants scared off them."

ALIBI AND DR. MORELLE

ERNEST DUDLEY

NIGHTMARE

WILDSIDE PRESS

ALIBI AND DR. MORELLE

For more information on this or other Wildside Press books, please contact:

Wildside Press
P.O. Box 301
Holicong, PA 18928-0301
www.wildsidepress.com

One

Dr. Morelle eased his gaunt angular frame more comfortably and his hooded eyes turned from Gilbert Winterton K.C., to the man in the dock who stood with his well-fed figure erect, his expression confident. His face was round and smooth, with a clear skin and round blue eyes; he was wearing a dark blue suit expensively cut, which gave him the appearance of a successful business man.

He had enjoyed more success than failure, and he had never been associated with violence until now. Now he stood indicted on a charge of murder. The murder of a police officer. The case had proceeded on its normal, unhurried way through four days of speeches, cross-examination and conflicting evidence. Dr. Morelle had heard it all. The strong case for the prosecution, the ingenious defence, and he felt convinced the man in the dock was guilty; but he would not have attempted to prophesy the verdict of the jury. In his opinion the two principal witnesses were responsible for confusing the issue, their evidence had been sharply conflicting and must have raised doubts in most minds to the disadvantage of the case for the prosecution.

The man Colson was accused of the murder while on a breaking and entering enterprise in St. John's Wood. He had denied the charge. He had almost proved, if not quite conclusively, that he had not been in the vicinity during the time when the crime had been committed.

The prosecution's case was that he had obtained a small tradesman's van on which he had lettered the name of a North London provision merchant. He had arrived at the house in question during late afternoon, knowing the occupants were away. He had taken a basket of supposed goods round the back for appearance's sake and had got in by forcing a window. He had lifted a mink stole, some silverware and a jewellery case containing a necklace and diamond pendant valued at nine hundred pounds.

Returning to the van he had found a Police-officer waiting for him. There had been a struggle and the policeman had been knocked down, regaining his feet as the van started. Colson had swerved straight at him and the other had died from his injuries without regaining consciousness.

The firm of provision merchants had categorically denied that any of their vans had been delivering goods in the St. John's Wood vicinity at the time; and the principal witness for the prosecution, a mild, oldish woman living in a neighbouring house, who had been in the street just prior to the murder, had been definite that the firm's name had been on the van. She had recognized Colson as the driver because as she was passing her attention was drawn to him by the police-officer's presence, whom she overheard question him about a dirty number plate. She had seen no one else in the van, and she had thought it strange that goods should be delivered when she knew the occupants had just gone away. When she had reached her own house she had looked back to see the van driving away and the policeman lying in the gutter. Promptly she had dialled 999.

Witness for the defence, a street-cleaner who had been working further along the road, stated how he had heard a shout and a motor starting. He had seen someone lying in the road as the van raced towards him, and had stepped out in an attempt to stop it but had been forced to jump aside. He had been close enough to see the driver plainly as he went past. He had not recognized him as the man in the dock. The driver of the van, he had been positive, wore a thin moustache and a peaked cap. He was also reasonably sure there was a passenger next to the driver, a woman, he thought. He had been unable to take the registration number because the rear plate had been obscured by dirt.

A frown creased Dr. Morelle's lofty forehead. How reliable were the two witnesses? Each had differed in their story. The street-cleaner should have been able to make a reliable observation. He had attempted to stop the van. His impression of what he saw should have been gained when his attention was entirely centred on the vehicle and its driver. Yet he had failed to recognize him as the man in the dock.

The woman had been equally certain that she did recognize him, and that there had been no one else in the van. She did not remember the driver wearing a hat or cap, but she remembered hearing the policeman question him about the number plate.

Hers had been no more than a casual interest in the incident and the defence had suggested that she would not have recorded it with such vivid accuracy as that of the second witness who narrowly escaped being run down. But she recognized Colson as the driver while the street-cleaner did not. Who was right? How much of their observation was exaggeration? How much coloured by that strange mental aberration caused by the sudden realization that they were individuals of importance? Whose evidence had weighed the most with the jury? Dr. Morelle thought he knew.

Now the jury had filed back. They had been out precisely one hour and twelve minutes. Nine men and three women. Twelve ordinary people, in whose hands lay the ultimate fate of the prisoner. Every eye was on them as they reached their seats, the shuffle of their footsteps sounding startlingly clear in the heavy silence of the Old Bailey court-room. Someone coughed. Dr. Morelle from the corner of his eye saw a woman, without taking her gaze off the jury, fumble in her handbag for some smelling-salts.

Dr. Morelle allowed his gaze to wander abstractedly round the scene. The sombre oak panelling of the courtroom accentuating the pale faces of its occupants, the dash of feminine colour in the public gallery, the stiff pallor of collar and wig. His eyes fixed on the man in the dock. What moments had he lived through of interminable despair and hope during the past four days, while the story had unfolded and reached its climax? His story.

There was a rustle of documents pushed aside and the Clerk of the Court stood up, nervously fiddling with his pince-nez. In a dry, thin voice he said: "Members of the jury, have you considered your verdict?" The foreman, round-faced with beads of perspiration starting on his brow, licked his lips. His voice was scarcely audible.

"We have."

Pause.

Then slowly that thin, dry voice framed the words: "Do you find Brian Colson guilty or not guilty?"

The foreman's low-voiced but firm response: "Not Guilty."

And the woman with smelling-salts suddenly tipped forward, uttering a faint moan as she fell into an inert heap. A shuddering sigh seemed to move over the court, and Dr. Morelle saw the prisoner's hands tighten their grip on the edge of the dock until it seemed the bone of the knuckles would pierce the skin.

Two

That evening Dr. Morelle turned the yellow, rakish Duesenberg out of Harley Street and headed in the direction of Whitehall. It was a dismal night with a cold drizzle falling out of a lowering sky that appeared no higher than Nelson's Column. The windscreen-wiper carved a continuous panel of vision through which he could make out the huddled traffic moving against the background of sloping rain and looming buildings of Regent Street, the great shops masses of bizarre colour, the side-streets caverns of blackness. The car hissed round Trafalgar Square and then he was turning off Whitehall and into the small forecourt of the club. Parking-space was filling, but he nosed the Duesenberg into a position so that he would not have far to walk in the rain to the club entrance. In a few moments he stepped briskly into the warmth of the foyer, a uniformed porter appeared unobtrusively to take his hat and coat, and Dr. Morelle went leisurely into the bar.

The club was famous for its cosmopolitan membership, numbering explorers, scientists, lawyers, criminologists among some of its more distinguished members who made it their headquarters when in London. Its spacious rooms, lofty ceilings, tall windows, flavoured its atmosphere with an old world tranquillity. Even the bar retained this impression with its round pillars down the centre of the floor, carved ceiling, and two faded oil-paintings either side of the Dutch-tiled fireplace. The dark oak counter was a modern concession; but there were no stools on which members could perch, they either leaned against it or took their drinks to one of the small tables.

It was a little early for dinner and no doubt Gilbert Winterton had been fully occupied since the close of the trial early that afternoon. But he would show up in due course, he had been keen to suggest the meeting, almost as if, Dr. Morelle mused, his failure to win the case had made it imperative he should talk to someone. Was it merely that he needed to relax after the concentration and effort he had expended over the trial? Dr. Morelle nodded to the white-coated man behind the bar, and found a leather-covered corner chair. He took a Le Sphinx from his thin gold cigarette-case and lit it. He sipped the drink the barman had brought him, relishing the smooth flavour while his hooded eyes flickered across the headlines in an evening paper that someone had left on the table next to him. **COLSON NOT GUILTY!** the banner headline screamed.

Dr. Morelle's mind went back to the Old Bailey. The two witnesses, two different people coming forward with different stories about the same event. Swearing to the truth of what they had seen yet innocently confusing the issue. On such conflicting obscuration had hung a man's destiny. It was an exasperating and fascinating subject, and he was still mulling it over when Gilbert Winterton came in.

He was of medium height, broad-shouldered and running to fat. His sleek dark hair thinned at the temples and above the thick bulbous nose, the cut and thrust of the court still seemed to glint in his round eyes, as he greeted Dr. Morelle. The barman hovered about them. Winterton did not talk very much over drinks, he seemed to be unwinding himself, and every now and again he sighed and closed his eyes. Over dinner he relaxed and began to discuss the trial in almost impersonal tones. He felt that the case against Colson had been a cast-iron one which had melted in the furnace of the witnesses inconsistencies. The cut and thrust glitter returned to his gaze as he talked.

"You were present throughout, Dr. Morelle. You know his alibi was broken, that the van was seen outside his lodging-house a few days before the crime, that the planning and execution of the robbery bore his trade-mark, and the woman recognized him as the driver of the van. Yet the damned street-cleaner who should have been receptive to an accurate impression comes up with his denial that the driver of the van was him."

Dr. Morelle touched his mouth with his table-napkin. "I was not surprised at the jury's verdict. A confliction of such important evidence in the matter of identity would have been sufficient to create reasonable doubt in the minds of any jury. Although the judge was inclined to favour you in his summing up, he had a duty to perform in emphasizing the disparity."

The other nodded and drained his wine glass. "I knew what the result would be," he said. "But what is the answer?" He delicately operated on a piece of cheddar. He transferred the portion he had cut to his plate and began to butter a biscuit. Dr.

Morelle made no reply. "You might say," the other went on, "that counsel could be more careful in their cross-examination of witnesses. But that would be no remedy."

"It would appear a human frailty," Dr. Morelle said, "that those subjected to recall observations in the full glare of a police-court with the subsequent publicity, cannot be trusted, the past event is trimmed by their imagination."

"About time someone did some research on it, "Winterton said emphatically. "Contributory factors on the unreliability of witnesses, that sort of thing."

"It would prove an interesting if somewhat exasperating subject for study," Dr. Morelle said.

The library made a quiet, restful place after the clatter and bustle of the dining-room. Glass-fronted bookshelves lined the walls from floor to ceiling, the carpet was Indian, once rich and thick, but now sadly worn in places. There were three writing tables and a long oak trestle table under the window with neatly arranged copies of current magazines and newspapers. There were deep leather arm-chairs and two sofas and coffee tables nearby.

Dr. Morelle and Gilbert Winterton found themselves in a corner and were served coffee, Winterton leaning forward stirring thoughtfully and puffing a cigar, while Dr. Morelle favoured an inevitable Le Sphinx. The barrister had still not exhausted the subject of the conversation over dinner now that they were settled in the library.

"As I see it," he said, waving aside a feather of tobacco smoke, "we ought to know how and why two or even several truthful and sincere people can go into the witness-box and each give a completely different account of one particular and identical event." Dr. Morelle added a lump of sugar to his coffee. He glanced up to meet Winterton's gaze focused on him, and his enigmatic face suddenly lightened with an understanding smile.

"Are you hinting," Dr. Morelle said, "that someone like me should interest themselves in some sort of an experiment?" He dragged at his cigarette and a sardonic expression played over his gaunt features, one eyebrow was raised quizzically. "Can it be," he said, "that this is the motive underlying your invitation to me to listen to to-day's hearing, together with the delightful dinner which I have enjoyed this evening?"

The other gave a frank chuckle. "It would be right in your line," he said. "It would be a most interesting investigation and your findings would be of estimable value to every criminologist."

Dr. Morelle eyed the other speculatively, and then he said: "What kind of investigation do you envisage?"

Winterton beamed his delight at Dr. Morelle's intimated interest in the idea, and spread his hands in a vague gesture of helplessness.

"I have only a pretty vague notion at the moment," he confessed. "All I feel is more than ever that you are the one to handle it, but how to set about it—" He broke off with a shrug. "You have something of a reputation for having participated in many unusual investigations." He smiled broadly. "I'm sure this undertaking would hardly be out of your depth."

Dr. Morelle tapped the ash carefully from his Le Sphinx. "You pay me an undeserved compliment," he said, the hint of a smile flickering over his chiselled mouth. "I must admit to being intrigued, but how to go about the project eludes me for the moment."

"I suppose one should begin with some sort of a small committee," Winterton said.

"And," Dr. Morelle said, "as the enthusiastic originator I assume you would be prepared to serve?"

"I shall be pleased to make myself available as soon as you have organized a plan of action. I quite realize," drawing at his cigar, "that it's the organization which takes up so much time and I only hope all this hasn't caught you at a time when you've got something extra important on your plate."

Dr. Morelle stubbed out his cigarette. "You will be hearing from me," he said.

It was still raining when Dr. Morelle headed back to Harley Street, already planning his first move towards the investigation scheme Gilbert Winterton had initiated; he was visualizing a committee of four with himself as chairman. With the next couple of weeks clear of any important engagement, he told himself, the idea had come along at an opportune moment. He fancied it, he could see its potentials; and he could set the wheels turning without any delay.

As he turned the Duesenberg round Piccadilly Circus with the neon signs a flashing backdrop of colour against the cold patter of rain, the names of likely members passed across his mind. Winterton, of course, would supply a valuable viewpoint; and someone in the sociological-cum-anthropological bracket was an obvious idea. He wondered if he could persuade a Scotland Yard top-brass to take an active interest. He was looking forward to beginning work on it in the morning.

Three

The blue sky above the London rooftops looked washed clean and clear by the night's rain. The sunlight slanted through the window of Dr. Morelle's study and spotlighted Miss Frayle who sat at her desk opening the morning batch of mail. She had already arranged to spend the Easter holiday with a girl-friend; it was drawing near, and every day she wondered if Dr. Morelle looked like involving himself in some case which would result in her plans ending up in a complete shambles.

The sunshine and clear skies that morning had sharpened her anticipation, and she was anxious to set her mind at rest and discover if the mail contained anything likely to prevent her forthcoming holiday. But there was nothing of any importance, and she gave a sigh of relief as she went through the letters.

Presently she turned to her note-book, straightening her horn-rimmed spectacles, and relaxing in front of her typewriter. There were a few laboratory notes left over from yesterday to type, and she began to tap the keys as Dr. Morelle came in.

Miss Frayle looked up and immediately experienced a feeling of dismay. Suddenly the holiday looked remote, after all. In all her years as his secretary she had found it impossible to fathom his thoughts, his usual saturnine expression gave nothing away; but this morning there was a buoyant glint in his eyes.

"Anything important in the mail?" His gaze flickered over the correspondence she had placed on his desk.

"Nothing that requires urgent attention," she said.

He lit a Le Sphinx. He blew a smoke ring across the shaft of sunlight, and she could feel him studying her speculatively. Something was in the air, she knew it. "I don't want anything clamouring for my attention for the next few days," he said. "I am planning a not unimportant experiment."

Miss Frayle glanced at him over her horn-rims. "In the laboratory?"

He nodded. "The laboratory of Life. It's a social experiment. With people."

"Oh," Miss Frayle said. She wondered how long it would take and her thoughts flew to her blessed holiday. It wasn't looking so good. Not good at all.

He crossed to the window and stared out abstractedly, his gaunt profile dark and forbidding silhouetted against the light. A taxi hooted somewhere along Harley Street. He came slowly back and sat down behind his desk. "The trial I was attending at the Old Bailey, I assume you know the verdict?"

"He was found not guilty," she said. "He was jolly lucky, don't you think?"

"He had to thwart a difference of opinion between the two principal witnesses." There was a hint of mockery in his tones. "My experiment will concern those factors that contribute to the unreliability of witnesses. Gilbert Winterton's invitation to me to attend the case was not entirely unmotivated."

She blinked at him behind her spectacles. She had always tried to cultivate that outward show of immunity which concealed the surprise or shock, tenderness or indignation that a considerable part of Dr. Morelle's activities one way and another aroused in her; but she was never able to succeed one hundred per cent. She knew that he could read the puzzled surprise she felt as he looked at her now and she felt a blush creep across her face.

"For some reason, Miss Frayle," he said patiently, "it seldom happens that two witnesses interpret the same scene in the same way. I refer, of course, to the facts of a given situation."

Miss Frayle's nod conveyed complete understanding, although she knew that he was perfectly well aware that she hadn't the slightest idea what he was talking about. Sometimes she wondered why she went to the trouble of trying to deceive him.

"Either they imagine certain aspects of what they see," he was saying, "or it gives them an exaggerated sense of their own importance if they colour their observations with fictitious trimmings. Admittedly no one can be certain what aberration it is compels many to admit to seeing something that didn't happen, there may be several contributory factors; while there are individuals much too reticent to invite greater attention and publicity than they already receive in the more sensational criminal cases, and a confliction of evidence only draws them further into the limelight." He contemplated the end of his Le Sphinx, while Miss Frayle did her best to make her expression one of rapt fascination. "I shall attempt to fathom the reasons for such unreliability in those who are normally reliable."

"It all sounds most exciting," Miss Frayle said. "Only, I mean, how does one set about it?"

"Means will be devised, that is the first purpose of this committee I am envisaging." He got up restlessly, crushed out his cigarette and stood at the window, his hands clasped behind him. In the sunlight his dark-clothed figure, his gaunt lean face and hooded eyes gave him a strangely sinister appearance, like a bird of prey. "Put aside those notes for the moment," he said over his shoulder. "And take a letter. Take several letters, in fact, one after another, naturally, I have no wish to impose too severe a strain upon you." But he saw that she was not listening. "Are you all right, Miss Frayle?"

"I was thinking," she said.

"I see," he said.

"You know, Dr. Morelle," she said, "wasn't there something like this in Paris? Some experiment to do with checking on witnesses' truthfulness. Apparently they're just as bad in France."

"I'm sure no one would suggest that compulsive lying on the part of police-court witnesses is peculiar to this country."

"Or perhaps it was in America," Miss Frayle said. "I know I read about it or heard about it somewhere."

"Is it very important, in any case?"

"I was thinking that if you could find out, it might be of some help to you," she said.

He eyed her narrowly. "I am very well aware," he said through a puff of cigarette-smoke, "of the experiment to which you refer, which did in fact take place in Paris."

"I thought it was there—"

"And," he continued with increasing suavity, "it was already pigeon-holed in my mind to get in touch with the people concerned with the object of securing their co-operative help."

"Yes, Dr. Morelle." She stared at him, innocent-eyed, perfectly convinced that he had never heard of the Paris thing at all, or if he had, she had reminded him. Of course, he had pounced on the information, for there would be a great mass of helpful material to which he could refer for this experiment he intended to conduct for himself.

"Quite so," he was saying musingly, "I heard about it when I was over there last year; and because it was unusual and interesting, I fancied it might prove useful to remember it. I seem to recall that something like a hundred witnesses were tested for their accuracy and reliability. The findings were still being probed when I left." He began pacing up and down, and Miss Frayle sat pencil poised over her notebook.

"No doubt for my purpose," he said, "perhaps a modification or two will be indicated. But I'm sure it would be just as successful in London, or anywhere else for that matter."

Miss Frayle edged forward in her chair as Dr. Morelle began to outline the scheme as he envisaged it in his mind.

Four

The dingy office at the back was even more untidy than the shop. Ted Patrick wrote his name with his finger on a corner of Benson's desk. Patrick thought the bookshelves, the safe, the ramshackle sticks of furniture, the small opaque window and the boarded floor had never seen a broom or a cleaning rag.

Benson looked that way, too; a shrivelled figure of a man, his unkempt appearance, slow, painful-like movements gave the impression that he had one foot in the grave. He wore an old velveteen jacket that was a sanctuary for a variety of food-stains, a moth-eaten woollen waistcoat and a velvet bow-tie, the ends of which straggled down over his chest. He had a mean, scraggy neck, and grey stubble dominated his chin and cheek bones. His face was a thin dead-pan enlivened by a pair of sharp brown eyes that reflected the glitter of the stones and trinkets before him.

He leaned over the desk squinting through his eyeglass at the ring in his fingers. The brittle light from the angle-poise lamp, the only concession to comfort and modernity in the room, played on the stones in the ring which gleamed with flashes of blue, gold and red as he turned it.

Patrick waited patiently. Tall, slim-waisted with broad shoulders, he was a well-proportioned figure, his suit a pin-stripe dark blue, double-breasted; his hat a soft velour. There was an air of confidence about him which was empha-sized in the casual look on a soft-lined, handsome face that had been carefully smoothed with after-shave lotion. He looked out of place in the dilapidated room behind the pawnbroker's shop.

His eyes began to move again distastefully over the odds and ends of rubbish cluttering the place. The broken pack-ing-case in the corner with a froth of straw protruding from the hole in its lid, the old heavy volumes on the shelves with the gilt lettering on their spines faded with age, the arm-chair with its soiled linen cover; only the safe looked substantial. It lodged be-neath a rough deal table against a bare wall, partially screened by a strip of coconut matting.

Patrick reflected on the difference between himself and the

man who owned and lived in this unsavoury joint. But he wasn't thinking of the difference in appearance or habit. It was the difference in cash. Benson stank with money. Patrick was broke.

The ring was a memento of his first job. He'd kept it through the years maybe with some subconscious intention of giving it to the right girl if he was ever tempted to settle down. He knew it wasn't worth a lot. That was another reason why he'd never cashed it with his other hauls. But now it was a case of having to. He'd been down for a short stretch. Now he was out and in circulation again, but the few weeks he'd been free had bored a big hole in his small savings. Nothing had turned up that was safe and attractive. Now he needed a few quid to settle his rent and other odds and ends and carry him around while he ferreted out the next job. He had to get moving.

He pushed his hat nonchalantly to the back of his head, and opened the envelope of silver which was his cigarette-case. He wasn't feeling so confident as he looked, but he had to put on a front for Benson's benefit. If Benson thought he was skint he'd cut his price to the bone. He knew Benson. A greedy codger. He never did like doing any business with him. The little pawnbroker was a fence, but Patrick also had a suspicion that he was an informer. So he always played safe with Benson. If he wanted a tenner he'd flog something that wasn't suspect. No case history. Like the ring. It wasn't too valuable and had been in his possession so long there were no strings to it.

Patrick slipped the cigarette-case into his pocket and leisurely lit the cigarette as Benson put down the eyeglass. The older man's eyes fixed him in a cold stare.

"Small fry," he said, holding up the ring so that the light glittered on the three diamonds inset in the metal. "The stones are not well-cut and the largest is no more than a half carat, the ones on each side a quarter." He paused. "I might have a sale for it. How much?"

"A hundred," Patrick said without hesitation.

"You're crazy like a fox." A gurgle of amusement welled up from somewhere in his throat and broke through the thin lips. "Where did you get it?"

"I bought it for my girl."

"She discovered its value and gave it back, eh?"

Patrick felt like wiping the grin off the face, but he couldn't afford that pleasure. He switched on a grin himself, looked unconcerned. "Nothing like that. Our relationship didn't work out, that's all."

"How much did you pay for it?"

"Hundred and fifty."

"Someone certainly saw you coming." He studied the ring again. "It's worth no more than fifty to me."

Patrick swallowed hard. He knew the fat profit Benson was after, and he wasn't going to give it away. But he also knew that he wouldn't better Benson's offer anywhere else. He had to bargain. He would get the price up if he played his cards right. He still kept it casual.

"You know you'll find a customer who'll treble your measly offer. But if that's your final figure, we're wasting our time. I'll take it elsewhere." He stretched out his hand for the ring. But Benson didn't appear to think he was wasting his time. He turned the ring round and round in his fingers, sucking in his breath noisily.

"You in trouble again?" he said without looking up.

"No. I'm just an ordinary, law-abiding citizen at the mercy of sharks."

Benson allowed himself a long, patient smile. He didn't react to the inference. "Need some money?"

"No more than anyone else needs it," Patrick said casually.

Benson put the ring down on the desk.

"Seventy is my limit," he said unexpectedly. "Not a penny more. I risk losing it at that."

Patrick frowned down at his cigarette. He gave the impression he was doing mental arithmetic. He was pleasantly surprised at the leap in price Benson had suddenly made and he had already calculated that he'd never better it elsewhere, but he wasn't ready to clinch the deal yet. His eyes moved over the other's face and his lips smiled.

"Now you're being reasonable," he said pleasantly. "I'll take eighty."

Benson shook his head. He started to get up from the soiled leather chair behind the desk. His stony expression relaxed a little and he glanced curiously at his visitor. "You got a cigarette?"

Patrick pulled out his case. Benson took a cigarette and then took the case. He put it under the lamp and examined it. He looked at the silver hall mark through his eyeglass.

"Asprey. Always marketable." He put the glass down and slowly raised his head. "You greatly attached to it?"

Patrick concealed his surprise. He thought he was getting the angle. Benson was looking for a way to boost his offer without giving in.

"Depends what you'd attach to it," Patrick said. It had been a present for a favour he'd done. He could get along without it. Right now cash was more important than goods. He watched amusedly as Benson ran his eyes greedily over the cigarette-case. Then he put it down next to the ring and brought out a roll of notes from his trousers pocket.

"Tell you what," he said. "You came here with the intention of leaving a hundred the richer." He began to peel off fivers. "You'd expect to drop ten per cent on any deal. I'll give you ninety pounds for the two."

It was inviting. The crisp fivers would carry him over the next six weeks. He could square up the odds and ends and live comfortably while he picked his next job. But he didn't see why he should let Benson take the candy without some sort of squawk.

"You got a thing about a round hundred, haven't you? You want two valuable objects for less than the price of one."

The other shook his head. "My final offer. Take it or leave it." He began to roll up the notes.

Patrick dropped his cigarette-stub on the floor and squashed it with his shoe. He reached over the desk and took another from his case. "I'll take seventy in fives and the rest in singles."

A few minutes later he stepped out of the shadow of the pawnbroker's shop and crossed the narrow street into the sunlight. A short walk brought him into Shaftesbury Avenue. He turned left and strolled in the direction of Cambridge Circus. The March breeze was light enough to leave the dust in the gutters. There were few people on the pavements, most of them were in the offices and shops flanking the street, but the road was busy with passing buses, taxis, private cars and vans.

Patrick had little attention for his surroundings. The sun and the mild air made him feel good, but the real reason for his peace of mind was the comfortable bulge of his wallet inside his jacket It wasn't a fortune, but it would tide him over. He'd get organized in the next few days, but the cash he'd got out of the pawnbroker would allow him time to be discreet, to avoid any risks; it would give him valuable time to prepare the ground.

He'd never expected to dig out a hundred that morning. He'd put the limit at seventy-five; but he'd made another fifteen and all he'd lost was a cigarette-case. The few extra quid were more important to him now. Cigarettes came in their own packets.

He waited for the traffic-lights to change at Cambridge Circus before crossing to the roundabout. There were more people here, moving along the Charing Cross Road and seeping out of the labyrinth of streets and alleyways that fed Soho. The early lunchers heading for the cafés and coffee-bars; little groups of men, some white, some olive-skinned, talking on street corners; others browsing in the windows of the bookshops in Charing Cross Road; pretty girls in high heels and smart clothes passed purposefully on their way to be stared after by the idle men.

The lights changed and Patrick waited for a Rolls-Royce to glide past his feet and without as much as a second glance at it he moved across to the roundabout. The great façade of the Palace Theatre threw its shadow over him and just beyond he glimpsed the Casino Cinema announcing the wonders of Cinerama. He continued down Shaftesbury Avenue towards Piccadilly Circus. As he drew nearer the focal point of the West End the traffic became thicker, the pavements more crowded. He had taken the route without any particular purpose, but now that he had come so far he realized the subconscious urge had led him towards his favourite bar. He had got something to celebrate.

He turned into Great Windmill Street, passed the famous theatre where the inevitable groups of men were peering at photographs outside, and on up the street to a little pub sandwiched between a block of shops and offices. He went into the bar and stood looking around for any faces he knew.

The place was not crowded. The half-dozen stools at the bar were occupied by four men and a couple of girls. There were three or four regulars sitting at the tables and another pair standing at the further end of the counter. But it was the girl sitting on her own in the corner who attracted his attention. She was a blonde, and a dark, smartly-cut suit smoothed the curves of a model-girl figure. The upturned nose and the large hazel eyes were familiar and when they suddenly focused him, he recognized the old invitation in her smile.

He started across to her, trying to recall the last occasion they'd been together. He thought it must be a year since they'd had that last fling before he went abroad. It had been fun, until she wanted to tie him down, then he'd discreetly broken it up. The trip abroad had saved him. And now here she was, attractive as ever and looking like she was in the money, and giving him the old come-hither look. Maybe she'd done well for herself. Maybe they could get together again to mutual advantage. He reached her table and took her hand. She squeezed it affectionately.

"Hallo, hon," he said.

Five

She was thrilled to see him. Patrick slid easily into the role of the attentive male, while behind the handsome smile and the bold eyes he was weighing up the advantages the meeting might bring. He was curious and he had to play the prodigal boy-friend until his curiosity was satisfied.

Her name was Myra Campbell, and she was drinking gin-and-lime. He told her to knock it back and join him in celebrating their chance encounter. He bought her another and treated himself to a lager. He was quick to notice the way she looked at him as he ambled to the bar. He hadn't forgotten that look. It had the dewy-eyed, I-surrender-dear touch about it. He came back with the drinks and a packet of cigarettes. When he had lit hers and then his own he was ready to get down to business. But she cut in first.

"You look prosperous, Ted." She moved a little closer. "What are you doing now?"

"Same caper," Patrick said casually as though it bored him to talk about himself.

She glanced down into her glass and when she looked up again the sparkle had gone out of her eyes.

"It's a mug's game," she said quietly.

He shrugged. "But what can you do? They won't let you go straight."

She stared at him.

"But you got a job. You went to Canada?"

"Sure, I went to Canada. But there was no job. I was led up the garden. The agency that sponsored me and fixed up the terms went bust when I got there. There wasn't even enough to pay my passage back. They were crooked, too."

He gave it her with feeling and she swallowed it. He never went to Canada. He'd gone to New York. It was a quick trip though he hadn't told her so. It was one way of breaking off the entanglement she'd started to weave around him. And the trip had paid well. But there'd been no steady job. It had been a simple smuggling assignment for the mobster out of whom he'd got the cigarette-case now marked with a ticket in Benson's window. That plus. But he wasn't going to tell her that, or about the silly mistake he'd made when he'd got back which sent him down for six months. It would spoil the reunion. She'd always hankered after the straight and narrow. She had got herself on it now. She was on the legal pay-roll. He was sure of that.

"What did you do then?" she asked.

"Tried to play it straight," he said. "But it was no dice. So in the end I did a little job in Toronto and hoofed it back." The lies slid off his tongue as smoothly as the tide-washed sand on a summer's day. He pointed to her glass. "Tip it back, hon."

She half-smiled a protest.

"Have to take it steady. Not drinking so much now."

"You've got room for a little one, I know. Come on. Then we'll get a bite to eat."

She finished the drink and he ordered another and took a double whisky himself. A glow of self-satisfaction warmed his veins. He still held some fascination for Myra. Even if it didn't open up a business avenue it would be fun to spend the day with her. Maybe make a night of it, too. He glanced at her, wondering where she was living, and who with. It gave him a pleasant glow to bathe himself in her admiring eyes. He deserved a break.

His gaze lingered over her as he returned to the table. She had nice features. Her mouth was small with full lips which glistened red over small, even teeth. The round eyes and up-tilted nose gave her a kittenish look. Her breasts were round, well-formed, adding a seductive curve to the jacket of her suit that hugged the slender waist. Her expensively stockinged legs were even more shapely than he'd remembered them. Maybe he should forget business and have a bit of fun. Snag was she was a serious girl. She'd got a thing about him and he couldn't risk repeating the situation from which he'd escaped a year ago.

He sat down, his eyes flashing invitations at her over his glass.

"You look healthy, hon, as well as beautiful," he said. "The colour of the rose in your cheeks. What you been doing with yourself?"

She giggled at him. "It's all this fresh air. I'm living down in Suffolk."

He glanced down at her hand.

"You married a farmer or something?"

She giggled again. "I'm not married. I'm working there. Little place called Hickham."

"Never heard of it."

"Between Newmarket and Bury St. Edmunds. You know Newmarket?"

"Who doesn't? You see plenty of gee-gees?"

"Sure." She paused to take another cigarette from the packet he offered her. "Mr. Hull's got some horses. They're over at Newmarket."

"Hull?" He was turning the name round and round in his mind. It was a familiar name. Connected with sport. Of course. He stared at her with a new interest but he was careful not to let it get into his voice. "Jimmy Hull, the famous sportsman? You work for him?"

"That's right," she nodded, smiling. "The lolly's all right and a good bit of time off. It's my day off to-day. That's why I'm up here."

He glanced slowly round the bar.

"Giving our old haunts the once-over eh?"

"Not all of them, Ted," she said quietly. "But I always look in here when I come up." She lowered her eyes, fingering the stem of her glass. "Thought we might run across each other again."

He spread his hands. "So now we have. So we're fated, that's what we are, hon. And we'll make the best day of it you've ever had." He rolled the whisky around his tongue savouring the warm taste of it. An idea was taking shape at the back of his mind. It wasn't a particularly original idea, but none the worse for that. An old idea was the best, he always said, especially if you could give it a new twist.

He drained his glass. "I should have come here more often," he said. "We'd have met up before."

"How long have you been back from Canada?"

"Couple of months," he said. "Been in here about a dozen times. Picked the wrong day every time. Except to-day." He watched her finish the drink, then he said: "If you're all set we'll go."

He took her to a small, cheapish little dump in Greek Street. It was one they had used sometimes in the old days. Soft seats, drapes and subdued lighting. There was a private room or two upstairs. The food was Italian, the wines good and reasonable prices. They didn't go upstairs, they found a corner-table. The place wasn't very full. She chatted away, skilfully prompted by him.

She had a day and three afternoons off in each fortnight; she came up to town once a month. She was Mrs. Hull's personal maid. There was a housekeeper who lived out and a daily woman. Hull himself employed a chauffeur-valet who lived in a flat over the garage. Mrs. Hull was something of an invalid, the nervy and anxious type, but it did not stop her travelling around with her husband, wintering in the Caribbean or on the Riviera. Myra had joined them there the previous autumn. She'd left a job in Nice. They'd be at Hickham Hall now for the next few months and Mrs. Hull, who always found it necessary to take sleeping-drugs, kept her jewellery upstairs.

It all took shape in Patrick's mind as he listened to her, and already the plan was forming. It was a natural. He couldn't miss. Would she fall in with his scheme, if he made the reward enticing enough? In terms of cash wouldn't be any good so far as she was concerned. He'd have to make it a promise of a trip abroad with a rosy future for them together.

Over the coffee he started to go to work. He took one of her hands. "You got yourself a regular job, hon, but you're still as elegant as a countess," he said with admiration. "Work hasn't spoiled your looks. In fact, it's good for them. I must try it myself sometime." He laughed, and she joined in, but her eyes had clouded a little. She was never one for much of a sense of humour, he remembered.

"I take care of myself," she said softly. "The work's okay. It's my nerves that get worn a bit. She's a bit of a needler."

"Just as well they're on the generous side with time off," he said, solicitously. "Gives you a chance to relax."

"I suppose so," she said dreamily. She looked at him. "I've got to wait a fortnight before getting around to seeing you again." She held his hand tightly. "Just like old times, Ted, isn't it?"

He nodded, he brought his face close to hers.

"It doesn't have to be a fortnight," he said. "When's your next free afternoon?"

27

"Friday."

"That's only three days ahead. We could meet then."

"But I'd hardly have time to get up here."

"You don't have to. I'll come down." His eyes searched her face. "That's what I'll do. Drive down in my car. We'll spend the afternoon together. Be a change to get some fresh air."

She was thrilled to bits. They went to a film after lunch. In the darkness of the cinema they squeezed hands, they pressed their knees against each other's, and he slipped his arm around her waist. It reminded him of his first date. He was too old for the teenage stuff, but he had to play his part. Myra was an incurable romantic. Afterwards she enthused over the picture, went over the plot with him, and while he said yes and no, he couldn't remember a single thing about it. His mind had run on other things while the film ran on the screen.

Over tea in a café just off Leicester Square, he was quick to notice when she began to glance frequently at her watch. She quietened down suddenly as if the spirit had gone out of her. He pushed his teacup towards her.

"Give us another re-fill," he said gently, "and tell me what's flown in and bitten you. Why so quiet and time-conscious?"

She poured the tea. A wistful little smile touched her lips and vanished. Her eyes were soft but they focused him steadily. "I was just thinking, it's been such a wonderful day," she said. "And my train goes in an hour."

"There must be another."

"I always go back on the same one. The chauffeur meets it for me."

"The posh treatment, eh? Very nice, too." Patrick smiled and spoke lightly. But she didn't smile back at him.

"Wish I didn't have to go back." She was wearing the wistful look she used to go in for in the old days. "You've unsettled me, Ted."

"I don't want you to go either," he said, with a sincere throb in his tone. "I've enjoyed this day as much as you. More even." He picked up his teaspoon and began to doodle with it absently, staring down at the coloured tablecloth. "We're both unhappy, and we needn't be. We've got a right to enjoy life as much as the next man or woman."

"But you never looked unhappy, Ted." Her eyes widened

with surprise.

"You have to put on a front," he said. "You don't wear your heart on your sleeve. It's only when you're alone or with someone you care about that you can let your hair down." From the corner of his eye he noted with satisfaction the expression on her face. Encouraged, he continued in the same low, confidential tone: "I'd like to quit this racket and settle down. I've been thinking about it lately and I've reached the same conclusion as you, Myra. It's a mug's game."

She put her hand over his, her eyes bright with tenderness.

"Ted, darling, you don't know what it does to me to hear you say that. To know that we've both got the same thoughts. We could start again, Ted, just where we left off. We could settle down in a place of our own, have a family, just like millions of others. Oh, Ted."

He wondered why she always used his name so much when she became emotional. He had teased her about it in the old days. But he didn't crack any joke about it now. "That's the only worthwhile thing." He looked at her affectionately. "That's how I'd like to see us. You and me. But it's not so easy to start again from scratch; to do it in the right way; and it's the only way to be sure of your happiness."

"What way is the right way, Ted?"

"I been thinking about it some time now. Turning it over in my mind." He stared down at the table again, a distant look in his eyes, as though he had projected himself into the future. "You don't stand a chance of going straight and settling down without money. You've got to give yourself a start. You and me never had a start. We owe it to ourselves. I owe it to you."

"Go on, Ted." she said quietly.

"Remember the Canadian job?" he said, "I played straight and what did they do to me? I tell you, you've got to rely on yourself. If you've got the money to start you off you don't need to worry about anyone else. So I've decided to pull one more big job. One last job to set me up and then I've finished with the racket. Forever."

She didn't say anything. She was looking down into her empty tea-cup as if she was trying to read her future in the tea-leaves. She was a bit superstitious. He remembered that, too. Horoscopes and that kind of junk.

"It's as simple as that," he said. "It would have to be something good. As little risk as possible. That's what I'm intending to go for. And then off to the South of France, or maybe Spain, somewhere where it's warm. Settle down, play it straight, with a little business. Export-import, something like that." He smiled at her. "How would you go for that, hon?"

"Sounds wonderful," she murmured. "Only it's—getting the money in the first place, I don't like. And without the chance of being caught."

"You've got to pick the right job," he said. "And you've got to work on your little ownsome. No one to blab, that's where the risk is. Besides, there're too many to share the loot. Now, someone like you and me, just the two of us, that would be different. We've both got the same objective. It's one final job with a means to an end. I want to quit the hole-in-the-corner stuff. You oughtn't to be slaving for the idle rich. We could go a long way together, Myra, just the way you want to go. All we need is the money to launch ourselves."

"You make it sound so smooth and simple, Ted," she said thoughtfully. "But how much money would we need?"

"A few thousand," he said casually, and lit two cigarettes and handed one to her. "Not worth the risk for anything less. And while you're about it you may as well take the best pickings you can."

She nodded, frowning a little. He could tell he'd sold her on the idea. She was seeing it the way he wanted her to. To go off with him and settle down. She was picturing it all. He could see it there, all across her pretty face. It made him feel good. His old charm was working. But he had to go steady with the final card. Be sure he won the trick.

"Been looking for the right thing to come along," he said. "Seeing you again has convinced me that quitting this racket and settling down is the only way for me from now on."

"What do you call the right thing?" She spoke quietly but there was a note in her voice which encouraged him.

"Oh, I dunno, hon," he said slowly. "But since we've been discussing him and he's loaded to the ears, I call the right thing something like Jimmy Hull." He watched her closely. She didn't bat an eyelid. He could hear the low hiss he made as he drew some air down into his lungs. He began to relax a little.

"She wouldn't miss the odd necklace," she said, her voice was suddenly cold. "All her stuff is insured anyway. I know just how I could let you in. And after the panic had died down, I could give my notice and join you." She stared at him eagerly. "Is that what you mean, Ted?"

It was precisely what he meant. He took a drag at his cigarette and gave a casual shrug.

"I dunno," he said. "But something like that, I suppose."

"You think we could get away with it, Ted?"

"Like water off a duck's back," he said, oozing with confidence. "You and me together, there's nothing we couldn't do."

It was difficult even now that he knew she was in his hands for him to believe his luck. It had gone as smooth as silk. The dice were running for him. Flogging his last assets to Benson must have started it. "We'll get a taxi to Liverpool Street and we'll have time for a drink before you catch the train."

"It's you and me together, Ted," she said softly. "But— this is for keeps? Eh, Ted?"

He squeezed her hand.

"For keeps, hon," he said.

Six

Ted Patrick climbed the stairs with a light step. He carried a bottle of Scotch and a pocketful of dreams, and the dreams were more realistic, more enticing than Myra's kisses just before the train had steamed out of Liverpool Street station.

He had come straight back to Stanhope Mews, collecting the Scotch *en route*. He had an evening's work to get through and he was anxious to get settled down to the job over a drink and a smoke.

He pushed open the door at the top of the short staircase, switched on the light and glanced round the living-room with a good-humoured sigh. It was a crummy joint, yet it was somehow cheerful. There was a small dining-table with ugly scratches across its oak surface, but the wood still gleamed in the light. A sideboard fitted snugly into a recess on one side, a couple of wild-fowling prints decorated the cream walls and by way of contrast, over the inset electric fire, was a lavish-looking print of a nude French girl by Domergue. He had seen it in a Continental glossy magazine and framed it in an amorous mood quite a while ago.

A cretonne curtain parted one-third of the room and behind it was a dressing-table and a wall cupboard and a divan-bed. Opposite the entrance from the stairs was the door into the small kitchen with the bathroom adjoining. It was a convenient place for him and the layout made the domestic tasks of cleaning and cooking simple ones. Stanhope Mews wasn't a bad address either. It gave him a West Two postmark and was a stone's throw from the Bayswater Road and about the same distance from Lancaster Gate Tube. It was not too central; but central enough.

He put the Scotch on the table and crossed to the window. The twilight had gone and the stars gleamed coldly. The mews was lost in shadow. The opposite block consisted of lock-up garages with store-rooms above. Further along a patch of faint light revealed a curtained window, but there were few residents in the cul-de-sac. No need to worry about being overlooked, but all the same he drew the curtains. That way he felt more comfortable.

He switched on the fire and opened the bureau which sided the window, carefully transferring into the drawer at the back the bulk of the fivers from his wallet. He locked the drawer, found a corkscrew in the sideboard and popped the cork of the bottle. He moved into the kitchen for a small jug of water. When he had mixed himself a generous slug and the cigarette was glowing, he settled down in the single arm-chair with a copy of the A.A. handbook. It wasn't the current issue. He'd never been a member. He didn't own a car. He'd gained his experience in other people's vehicles and the self-drive hire-firms. He had picked up the book in one of these cars the previous year for future reference. Now he thought it should help him to get acquainted with the area in which he was going to operate.

He turned up Bury St. Edmunds. It was in West Suffolk. A municipal borough with a population of twenty-thousand odd. It was seventy-five miles from London, twenty-eight from Cambridge, forty-three from Chelmsford and fifteen from Newmarket. It didn't tell him much, but he guessed it was an historical place. He was going to meet Myra there at three o'clock in the square called Market Hill close by the Abbey gardens.

He flipped the pages to the Hs; but Hickham wasn't mentioned. It was too small a place. He leafed through to the map section and found the region from London to the Norfolk border. He traced over the main routes with his finger. The A.11 out through Woodford, Epping and Bishops Stortford to Newmarket was the clearest and probably the fastest route to Bury St. Edmunds, but he wondered if it wouldn't be safer to go the slightly more roundabout way through Chelmsford, Braintree and Halstead and then via Sudbury.

He could take the journey at a leisurely pace when he went on Friday morning and note the route for when he made the final trip. He'd have to swipe a car for the job and dump it afterwards. Somewhere not too far from a main line railway-station. The bigger the town, the more travellers, the more trains. His eye moved a fraction over the map. A place like Ipswich, for instance. He turned back to the directory. Ipswich was twenty-six miles from Bury. Add on another five or six miles from Hickham and he'd have about thirty miles to travel before dumping the car.

He squinted at the page through a puff of cigarette-smoke, then he pushed the book on to the table and sipped the whisky. He couldn't plan that end in detail till he had a map of Suffolk. That would be the first item on his shopping-list in the morning. Scrupulous planning was the keynote to success. Any fool in the business knew that. Yet it was surprising the number who slipped up on details. He'd done so himself. But this time, and the co-operation of a devoted inside contact the other end...

He grimaced smugly into the whisky glass. Myra had swallowed his act hook, line and sinker. It was a pity to disappoint the kid, but he'd got to think of himself. It was no time to be sentimental. He'd see she got something out of it, but by the time she was ready to join him at the end of the mission, he'd have cashed the loot in Amsterdam and be on his way through Europe. But that was the near future. The present was sufficient to occupy his mind.

He knew he could rely on Myra to prepare the set-up her end. The layout of the house, the time, the entry; they'd work that out together on Friday. And then he'd put up for the night somewhere and plan his getaway route in detail and a means of disposing of the car. Meantime, the organization his end was straightforward. He'd hire a car for three days. And on his way through the eastern suburbs on Friday morning he'd look out a likely haunt for picking up a suitable car for the job.

He knocked the ash from his cigarette and took a deep drag, turning over in his mind the other very important item in his plans. An alibi.

His alibi would have to be good. Watertight. The police knew him. However smoothly the job went there might be questions. It would be routine stuff, but he'd got to have a ready answer. A convincing one. Something that would have proved him to be right here in town.

He dropped the cigarette stub into the ash-tray as it began to heat his fingers and poured himself another drink. He settled back in the chair again, his hands clasped under his chin, his fingers moving restlessly across his mouth. The alibi was going to be the most difficult part. His eyes moved slowly around the room while his mind searched for an idea. He got up and padded around the flat.

It was an advertisement for a film in the previous day's issue of the *Evening News* that set his mind working along the right track. He suddenly remembered Harry Price.

The newspaper lay folded on the sideboard. He noticed the splash announcement with an action picture and the names of the stars who headed a cast of thousands. Extras, that's what they were. That's what Harry Price was. Patrick had met him a couple of years earlier at the film studios at Elstree during a period when he had tried his hand at an honest job.

They had been extras in a crowd scene in some mammoth production. At least it was called a mammoth production. Since Price lived nearby in Paddington they'd met on occasions after their work on the film finished. Patrick had hastily given up this unprofitable diversion from his normal routine; extra work on films was too chancey, but Price managed to carry on a precarious existence.

He was always short of cash and was thus ever-ready to make the easy shilling. Maybe he could provide the alibi.

He and Price were similar in build and appearance. A little dressing-up and an odd dab of make-up and Price could pass off for him, provided the scrutiny wasn't too severe. He lived in Talbot Square off Sussex Gardens. It wasn't far, and it was a nice night for a walk. It would be comforting to get the alibi settled.

Patrick emptied his glass and rose leisurely to his feet. He hoped Price would be pleased to see him.

Patrick met no one he knew. It was just after nine and the streets were quiet apart from the occasional purr of a car or taxi. Sounds of conviviality seeped through the windows of the pubs he passed and their lights threw splashes of colour across the pavements. The March wind was cool but there was no strength in it. The whisky and the sweet feeling of anticipation filled his veins. He knew the Hull job was going to be the plum of his career, the chance of a life-time. He'd be able to afford to quit the racket and settle down, though not exactly in the way Myra envisaged.

He crossed the wide street of Sussex Gardens and headed along the pavement towards Talbot Square. A faint hiss of steam reached him from an impatient engine in Paddington Station. It conjured up a picture of first-class travel, posh hotels, lazy days on summer beaches. That was the life. And he could reach it, now.

He turned into the square. He hadn't been to Price's place for some time, but he remembered it clearly. It was on the top floor. Quite a comfortable set-up which he thought Price must find difficult to maintain. It was small and it wasn't luxurious, but he wondered where the rent came from. Not that it was any of his business. He was just a bit concerned by the possibility that Price might be temporarily in the money at the moment or engaged on a lucrative job, and would turn down the proposition he was about to offer.

When Price let him in he could tell that he'd done nothing very profitable for quite a while and hadn't much lined up for the future.

Now that he was looking for points Patrick noted with satisfaction how Price had the same dark wavy hair, the same colour eyes and the same dimple in the chin. A difference in the bone-structure of the face, Price's cheek bones being higher and more prominent than his own. The line of the nose was smoother too. But to the casual observer it would be easy to mistake these characteristics, and with a touch or two of make-up and the right clothes it would take more than a cursory glance to identify who was who.

Price was wearing a shabby sports coat and soiled grey flannels. His shirt was creased and overdue for the laundry. The room was sparsely furnished and Patrick wondered if the bailiffs had been in. One element of the two-bar fire was aglow and close to it was a chair and a small table.

Price pushed the one remaining chair in the room towards the fire. It was an old leather arm-chair and Patrick could see that the springs had gone. He sat down on the arm.

"Long time no see," Price said. "What brings you here at this hour?"

"Thought you might be interested in a little proposition I have." Patrick looked slowly around the room.

"Could be." Price spoke cautiously. "What is it?" He pulled out a crumpled packet of cigarettes and offered one. He struck a match. "Sorry I can't offer you a drink. Clean out. But they're not closed yet. We can have one at the local if you fancy it."

"I'd rather talk here." Patrick glanced round again. "How

you doing at the moment, Harry?"

Price shrugged and sat down in his chair.

"Things are a bit sticky." He grinned sheepishly. "You probably notice I've had to pop one or two items that were cluttering up the place." He began to shuffle some photographic prints he had on the table in front of him into an envelope. "No work for some time. Going through a bad phase with all this T.V. and stuff. Trying my hand at a bit of art."

He grinned again and held up one of the photographs. It was a picture of a nude girl leaning against a pattern of wrought-iron work. It was a typical studio job. "Be surprised at the demand for this stuff. Trying to muscle in, but it's depressing work." He pushed the print into the envelope with the others and dropped it on the floor. "What's this proposition of yours?"

"Just a little impersonation of me," Patrick said. "A few hours idling about in one or two of my usual haunts to give the impression I'm in town when I'm not."

Price jabbed his finger through a smoke ring he'd made.

"I get it. Out on a job, eh? You want me should provide the alibi?"

A smile flickered across Patrick's mouth but his eyes were cold.

"I make a practice never to go into details, when they're not necessary," he said. "It's liable to spoil everything and then there'd be no job or loot for anyone else. And right now I can't tell you exactly when, but it should be in the next week or so. You be free, Harry?"

"I could arrange it." Price looked at his burning cigarette speculatively. "If it's worth while. What's in it for me?"

"A tenner to start with," Patrick said. "If everything goes smoothly then, of course, there'd be a bit more."

"How much more?"

"Another fifty." Patrick gave him a broad grin. "Not bad for a few hours of idleness, eh?"

"You pay for the risk I take, Ted," Price suggested.

"I take the risk," Patrick said pointedly. "You loaf around and just collect." He got up and squashed his cigarette in the grate. "I'll fix you up with the clothes and give you the details when the time comes." His eyes strayed to the telephone on a shelf by the door. "I'll give you a ring soon as I'm ready. Maybe over the weekend."

Price rose, his hands in his pockets.

"Okay. I'll look forward to it." He accompanied Patrick to the door, but he didn't open it. "Just one thing, Ted," he said hesitatingly. "Since you've booked me, so to speak, and I've agreed to remain open for the date, how about a little on account, just to clinch it?"

Patrick nodded and opened his wallet. He counted out five pounds and handed them to Price. He noted the haste with which the other took them, and he grinned sardonically.

"Fair enough?" he said.

"Fair enough." Price sounded grateful.

Patrick went out into the night his mind contented. He was looking forward to the drive down to Suffolk on Friday.

Seven

The traffic thinned out east of Newbury Park. The double carriage-way of Eastern Avenue opened up before him inviting him to speed through outer suburbia, but he was taking it easy. He was content to nurse the Vauxhall along at a steady cruise. From now on, too, he had to keep his eyes peeled for a likely roadhouse or pub which he could earmark for his starting point on the night.

He had picked up the self-drive car that morning and had left Edgware Road just after nine. He felt satisfied everything was now organized his end. He'd studied the route and acquainted himself with the Suffolk roads he was likely to use from the map on the seat beside him. He'd dipped into a Suffolk guide-book and this was pushed under the dashboard.

All that remained was to plan the entry, the time and details of what he was likely to find ready to pick up at Hickham Hall. And Myra would have all the dope on that when they met in Bury St. Edmunds that afternoon.

He was pleasantly surprised at the way she had cottoned on to everything. He had experienced his moments of anxiety during the last couple of days. He had wondered if she would go through with it. Once she was back in Suffolk and could think the whole thing over on her own, could be she might start feeling panicky, want to back out.

Being on the straight and narrow the way she had the past months even his hold over her might have lost its grip once she was out of his company. But she was still keen. She'd even come through on the blower the previous evening to confirm their arrangement for that afternoon and had sounded quite excited. "I have already begun at my end," was what she had said. She expected to be able to tell him the time for the job and the general set-up when they met. It looked like being the easiest caper he'd ever latched on to.

He was so busy anticipating the result of it all that he almost missed the place he was looking for. It was a yellow metal sign swinging in a wooden gallows on the side of the road. Turn left three hundred yards ahead for the *Spinning Wheel,* the sign said.

Patrick slowed down behind a petrol tanker and, as the ponderous vehicle drew ahead he saw the roundabout. Beyond it on the opposite side of the road was a large modern service station complete with car showroom. It looked like what he wanted.

He changed down, turned left and drove slowly up a macadam road little wider than a lane. Trees and hedges on either side, and there were two or three fine detached houses standing back off the road in well-kept grounds. The *Spinning Wheel* lay back among some elm trees, its spacious car-park fronting the road. It was a low, modern white building and in the occasional splashes of sunlight that poured through gaps in the cloudy sky, the place had a lazy, summery appearance.

As he turned into it, Patrick could picture the park crowded with cars each night. Now there was one car and a delivery van. Close to the gate in the high wall leading into the gardens he noticed the car-park attendant's hut. It was empty. The man, he decided, only showed up in the evening.

He parked to one side of the building and sat in the car a few minutes taking in general appearances. The *Spinning Wheel* was two storeys with a shallow pantile roof in green. There were a couple of balconies just above and on either side of the wide entrance. There were windows either side of the front doors and he could see that those to the right looked out from a large bar. Over the wall of the gardens beyond he could see the frame structure of a diving-board. In the chill March wind, the thought of the open-air pool sent a shiver down his spine.

His eyes shifted round the almost empty park again. The chain fence dividing it from the road with three wide gaps in it for the entry and exit of vehicles; the couple of floodlights low down on the ground to light up the *Spinning Wheel* during darkness. But there were no lamps to light up the park.

It was coming up to ten o'clock, his watch told him. He slipped the ignition-key into his pocket, and got out of the car. He crossed to the door to his right. It was the saloon. He looked in. A long counter running the further side of the room and tables and chairs set out. It was a large, cheerful bar. Ahead of him a wide corridor, a staircase with a notice: Ladies' Powder Room. On the door to his left he read: Cocktail Lounge. He went in.

It was nicely furnished, all right. The carpet was good. The chairs comfortable. The *décor* was cream and pink. There was a small bar in the corner with a door in the wall behind it. The bar was closed up and there was no one in sight. Through a wide curtained archway close to the bar he could see into the dining-room and beyond that he glimpsed a larger room with a square of boarded floor and tables surrounding it and a shallow stage at the end.

He went over to the bell-push in the wall but before he reached it a girl came in. She wore a short black dress with a small lace apron, high-heeled black shoes and her hair was chestnut. She was about twenty and cute-looking.

"Coffee"?

She knew she was cute-looking. She had a nice smile, so he returned it with interest and nodded.

"Black or white?"

"Milk, honey," he said.

Her nose wrinkled and there was a kittenish twinkle in her dark eyes.

"Honey we don't have," she said politely.

He grinned at her and found a low chair and looked at her legs as she walked out. He picked up a magazine and idly turned the pages, but he was concentrating on the girl. He'd got to be casual, but he thought she'd play.

A minute or two later she appeared with a tray of coffee. She put it down on the small table in front of him. She leaned over holding the coffee-pot. She said conversationally: "Don't think I've seen you here before, sir, have I?"

"It's been my loss," he said. "This is new territory for me. It's not so easy to find your way around, but it's always interesting, travelling in new territory."

"Oh," she said, "you're a traveller then?" She sounded a bit disappointed.

"Represent a paint firm." He looked her up and down. "You got a nice line in a nice line yourself," he went on amiably. "I see you have dances here."

"There's plenty of life. Too much sometimes."

"Keep you on the go, eh?" he gave her a sympathetic smile. "How often?"

"The dinner and dances? Almost every night. One on to-morrow, always one Saturday night. And three next week. Monday night, Wednesday and Saturday again."

"What time they finish?"

"Midnight Saturday, but other nights it's one and two in the morning."

"You have to work that shift as well?"

"Only if they happen to be a bit understaffed." She gave him a sly glance. "I start at nine and I usually finish at six."

"That I must remember," he said. She smirked at him. He was going to remember it, but not in the way she was thinking. So there was no chance of being seen by her when he came on the night, he was thinking.

She said, and it was as if she was answering his thoughts: "I sometimes come along to dance with my boy-friend."

His glance caressed her face.

"Lucky boy," he said. He wasn't worried. He had no intention of going into the dance himself. She'd be too busy having herself a good time to notice him if he had to look into the cocktail-bar. He thought the set-up was perfect. There was just one other point he had to clarify. Maybe she could tell him.

He nodded in the direction of the car-park. "Doesn't seem to be a petrol-pump near. I suppose that garage down the road stays open late?"

She hesitated and when the frown lifted she said: "You mean at the roundabout? I don't think they keep open very late this time of the year. I think after Easter they're open till about eleven."

A bell buzzed somewhere and she hurried off. He drank his coffee. It would suit his purpose okay. He'd just have to check the garage and then he could get on his way. He poured another cup of coffee and drank it quickly. He wanted to get moving but not before he saw the girl again.

He got up and went and took a brief look into the dining-room and the dance-room. Then he came back and pressed the bell. He was standing by the window when she came in.

"Thought you'd prefer me to pay before I took off." She wrote him out a bill while he talked. "If I did manage to get around to looking in one of these nights do I have to wear my soup-and-fish?"

She handed him the bill, and shook her head. "They don't wear evening-dress, if that's what you mean."

He was smiling to himself as he got in the car. He drove out of the car-park and slowly down the road towards Eastern Avenue.

He pulled up before he reached the corner and lit a cigarette. He was eyeing the garage opposite. There were four pumps, and he could see a couple of white-overalled attendants. There was a driveway either side of the pumps and lining the inner one was the main building. He noted the small office and adjoining it a showroom to take three or four cars. He could see two through the windows but whether they were used or new he couldn't be sure from his position. One of the signs over the windows told him that the proprietor was agent for Vauxhall and Austin cars.

He took a long drag at his cigarette. There was nothing else in particular to note. He glanced at his fuel-gauge. The tank would take about three. He let the clutch in and drove on to the avenue, looking for the next garage.

About a mile down the road he saw it. A small business with two pumps. They pumped a brand of petrol different from the one at the roundabout. There was a workshop behind the pull-in and an old car in the process of breaking up at the back. It was a one-man show.

He swung off the road and stopped with his filler-cap close to one of the pumps. An overalled figure appeared from the workshop wiping his hands on a piece of cloth. He was obliging, wiped the windscreen before he worried about the order. Middle-aged, with a round cheerful face, Patrick guessed him to be the owner. He gave his order and as he paid the man he put the final question.

"What time do the garages in these parts close?"

The man fingered Patrick's crisp note.

"I close at seven, but I open six-thirty in the morning and eight on Sundays." He glanced along the road in the direction Patrick had come. "But the garage up at the roundabout, they're later. Half past eight they shut, eleven in the summer." He glanced the other way. "There's another service station about three miles along. Closes at eight They both open after me in the morning."

Patrick collected his change and swung on to the road once more. He'd got all his facts now. He was putting himself in the picture. The garage at the roundabout couldn't have been more conveniently placed to the *Spinning Wheel* and it shut up shop at exactly the right time. He could safely pigeon-hole the idea he'd worked in his mind until the time came to put it into operation.

He settled down to enjoy the drive.

Eight

He crossed the county boundary of Essex and Suffolk just before entering Sudbury a few minutes after noon.

With only seventeen miles to go and nearly three hours to spare before meeting Myra in Bury, he thought his stomach and the time could be filled up at a pub in the old market-town.

From Gallows Corner, where he had turned off Eastern Avenue, he had taken the A.12. He had done that route before on more than one occasion as far as Colchester. But from Chelmsford taking him through the centre of Essex and Braintree and Halstead to the Suffolk border was a new experience. His observations along the way, designed for a particular purpose, eliminated any chance of his being bored with some of the comparatively flat country he passed through.

There had been no difficulty about memorizing the route. It had been straightforward and well signposted. He had decided to return over the same route to give his memory an opportunity of soaking up any useful details he might have overlooked on the way down; but he didn't think he'd have any identity troubles on the night drive. He had driven at a leisurely pace after leaving Chelmsford and had familiarized the few junctions, forks and turnings which he would have to recognize in the light of his headlamps.

From the long hill outside he had gained his first view of Sudbury. It lay sprawled across the valley with the River Stour a winding ribbon into the country on either side. Even under the cloudy, windswept skies, he could imagine it on a hot summer's day, the water-meadows below which fringed the western side of the town making a cool and inviting picture.

He coasted gently down the hill and went over the slight hump of the river bridge and along the narrow streets to the town centre. He parked on Market Hill in the shadow of St. Peter's. He got out, stretched, and walked slowly up past the church. He stared up at a bronze statue in front of the church, with brush and palette in its hand, wearing breeches and a long coat. He didn't trouble to see who the old geezer was, as he lit a cigarette and went in search of a drink and eats. He came to the Bell Inn and went in to the bar with its blackened beams and oakpanelled walls, and he ordered himself a draught beer. As he drank he studied the menu on the counter and he had worked out his lunch by the time he went into the small dining-room.

He left Sudbury before two o'clock so there was still time to dawdle, and once he'd cleared the town, traffic was very light. The sun came out and warmed the interior of the car through the windows and he began to feel as sleepy as the places he passed through. He opened the ventilating window and pulled down the door window a bit to freshen himself.

Long Melford was the first large village he came to, one long wide street flanked on either side by a continuous row of houses, some timbered, some brick-faced, all differing from each other, and fronting direct on the street which had no pavements.

He pushed on, his mind concentrated with the loot that he reckoned was coming to him in the course of the next few days. He passed through a straggling hamlet, catching a glimpse of a distant hangar to his right on the disused airfield near the outskirts of Lavenham. The road ran straight ahead for some distance; now and again, to break up the monotony of the fields on either side, an isolated farmhouse or a pair of cottages.

Patrick drove slowly through another village; and then topping the wooded rise a few minutes after passing through Sicklesmere, he saw just ahead the outskirts of his destination. He glanced at his watch, lying flat on his thick, powerful wrist. It said two-thirty.

He cruised along within the town speed-limit and passed the outlying row of houses which brought him to a new roundabout. Negotiating this he noted the wide road leading off to his right was the route to Ipswich. He drove straight on through a short narrow stretch with terraced houses on either side and over a shallow rise where the road broadened.

He nearly overshot the **NO ENTRY** signs at the corner, the blind turning of the one-way street leading up towards the centre of the town was too narrow to appear so important. He was forced to reverse a few feet to get round. There was no traffic behind and he was able to change course quickly and drive round the long rising bend turning left at the top into Westgate Street. The street widened out and he passed the large buildings of a brewery but he was still outside the centre of the town.

He noticed he was sweating a little, it wasn't the exertion of handling the car. It was an undercurrent of excitement that had surged through him. He wondered idly if his nerves were steady as they used to be. Prison did that to a man, undermined his nervous system. Even though he didn't know it, until too late. He passed some narrow streets which he thought must lead to the centre but it wasn't till he came to a fork in the road that he decided to turn. He swung round to the right just before the parting of the roads and entered the narrow one-way street. He slowed up at the junction where the street widened, passed the Corn Exchange and the town hall and pulled up on the Cornhill near the post office.

There was a large square to his right that led into another street on the further side lined with shops. He was sure he was in the town centre and he knew Market Hill could not be far away. He got out of the car and asked a man gazing into a shop window.

He started the car again and, following the man's directions, turned across the square and into the Butter Market. At the end he turned left and went down Abbeygate Street. He came out on the spacious Market Hill and saw the Abbey gateway to the gardens opposite. On both sides of him there were cars parked on the hill but part of the left-hand park was reserved for the single-deck country buses, and three were occupying it.

At the foot of the hill he turned right on to the road looking for a parking space. There was plenty of room further back and he swung round and up the slope stopping between the lines in front of the Angel Hotel. He remained in the car taking in the scene.

The square was busy with traffic and people. It was fringed by an assortment of buildings, dominated by the magnificent Abbey gateway some sixty feet high. It was flanked on either side by the old walls of the gardens inside.

It was coming up to three o'clock and he thought he should show himself. He didn't know from which direction she would appear, but he decided to get over near the gateway and Myra should see him easily enough.

It never occurred to him for a moment that she wouldn't show up.

He stood in the shadow of the gateway pretending to admire the richly decorated work, the heads and small carvings, canopied niches and traceried panels, slender clustered shafts and shields. A feeling of anxiety began to nag at him. He tried to understand what caused it, but couldn't put his finger on it. He lit a fresh cigarette and tried to relax.

He turned and came out on to the pavement as somewhere a clock struck three; and he saw her getting off the bus that had just pulled in opposite. She waved to him and hurried across the road to meet him. He was thankful she didn't wrap herself round him with a kiss. It wasn't wise to act too familiar in public, not so near the scene of operations, anyway.

"Waiting long?"

"You should remember, hon." He grinned with all his old confidence. "Always worked things on time." He took her arm, "But it's too chilly to hang about here. Let's get over to the heap."

They went across to the park. It was warmer in the Vauxhall. They relaxed on the front seat and Myra forgot to straighten her skirt. Patrick's eyes fastened on her knees and he had to jerk himself back to the business of the moment. She looked very pretty with her blonde hair awry where the wind had loosened it. His eyes focused on her face.

"Got things set up my end." he said. "How's it going this? You already been at work?"

"All fixed," she said tightly. He could see by her eyes and the way she gripped the clasp of her handbag that she was excited. Her words made sweet music in his ears, and he was anxious to know what the fixing was.

"What's the plan?" he asked, and then added lightly. "But before that maybe I ought to check with you if there is any stuff and if its get-at-able?"

"There's plenty. You won't be disappointed."

"Okay. You got a plan?"

"I sketched it out last night." She indicated her handbag. "The place will be wide open early Tuesday morning."

"Sounds okay, hon," he said. He remembered the dance at the *Spinning Wheel* Monday night. The date was perfect. It would give him nice time in which to get back to London to-morrow and fix up with Price on Sunday. He glanced out of the window and then back to Myra. "We'd better move off to some place quiet where we can talk. You can show me the layout."

She nodded, her eyes glittering. He thought she was as excited over the caper as he was. He smiled at her thinly.

"You took the words out of my mouth, Ted," she was saying. "I was going to suggest we go out to the house, drive past, just so you'll know the place. And it'll make it easier for you to follow my sketch. Then I know a place we can talk over tea."

They drove off Market Hill into Crown Street again. She was taking him on a route that would skirt the town centre, she said to him. She thought it might be handy for him to memorize it. After that he asked no more questions, but took note of the way and where they came out on to the A.45, the Newmarket road. They left the army barracks and the last few houses behind and once over the long hump of the railway bridge the fast Newmarket road began to open up.

About a couple of miles along she cautioned him to ease up and to take the turn off right at the next cross-roads. He slowed for the junction and as he swung the car round he noticed the signpost: Hickham 3.

They drove down a lane which in places was little more than the width of two cars. The land was a mixture of arable and pasture with here and there clusters of trees. Occasionally, a farmhouse would appear, lying back some distance off the road. He kept his eyes peeled all the time. On either side of the road for most of the way there was a grass verge, then a shallow ditch and beyond it a hedge which gave way to shrubs and young trees in one or two places.

"There's Hickham Church." She pointed to a square tower among a spray of elm trees. "We run into the village just after that. Hickham Hall is the other side." She took a scarf out of her bag and covered her head pulling the ends of it down over the sides of her face. She sank a bit lower in the seat.

"No one's likely to recognize me," she explained. "But best to be prepared."

He nodded. She was a good kid to be so careful. "What about your place? Anyone likely to be around as we go past?"

"No. Hull is out in the car. The chauffeur's with him. Mrs. Hull will be in the library having tea. The library looks out on to the back lawns. Kitchen is at the back, too."

She was right about the village, it was deserted. And they had passed the inn, the single store and post office and the half-dozen cottages within the space of half a minute. She sat up, but she kept the scarf on.

After the village the road curved two or three times. The hedges flanking it were tall but well trimed. He was wondering when they would come to it, when she spoke sharply.

"Easy, Ted. It's just round the next long bend."

He took his foot off the accelerator, and sat up over the wheel.

He was irritated to find he was sweating again

Nine

The house lay well back off the road partly screened by two big chestnut trees which stood either side of the centre path dividing the front lawns. It had a tall privet hedge that maintained a neat wall of green alongside the road. There were two pairs of double gates in wrought-iron which made an impressive entrance and exit for the drive each end of the frontage. The gates stood open.

Patrick drove past as slowly as he could without risking arousing curiosity, but there was only time to glimpse the ends of the house up each driveway. He could see the white wooden recessed frames of the top windows and the short steep roof over the hedge as he passed; but that was all. It was not as large as he had expected; but it was impossible to get an accurate impression of the place from a passing car. He told Myra so.

She agreed, but she knew it was too risky to hang around any longer while she was with him.

"I only wanted to be sure you knew the house," she said. "You can take a longer look before you go back to town, when I'm not with you."

"I'll do it in the morning," he said. "I'm staying the night in Bury." He pushed his cigarettes over to her. "Get the tobacco drawing. Can use one right now."

She lit two cigarettes and passed one to him. He had his eyes on the cross-roads ahead.

"Where we going?" he asked.

"Straight on, Barton Mills. Fowler's Inn is a quiet place. There'll be no one there now."

They drove on through another straggling village and overtook a policeman on a bicycle.

"Local cop?" Patrick said when they had passed.

She came up from low in the seat and began to loosen her scarf.

"This is all his beat," she nodded. She smiled and shook her hair as the scarf came away. "I guessed you didn't want an introduction."

"All I'm interested in is the introduction to that place," he jerked his head back in the direction they had come. "Don't you think I've waited long enough to hear your version of the routine, hon?"

"Sure you have, Ted." She was serious again. "It's quite simple. Hull and the chauffeur will be leaving the house five-thirty Tuesday morning. They'll be away all morning with Hull's trainer over at Newmarket. Hull just got himself a new horse, and it's coming down from Lincolnshire to the trainer's stables. Hull wants to see it put through its paces. That's definitely lined up."

"So the job can't be done till after five-thirty?" He frowned. "It'll be light then."

"Only just," she pointed out. "But there'll be no one to see you."

"What about the house? Who'll be in?"

"Mrs. Hull like I said, who sleeps like the dead. You don't have to worry about her."

He threw her a narrow glance.

"What makes you so sure?"

"It's my job to look after Mrs. Hull," she said. "You know that; and I already told you she's a bit of an invalid. She has to take sleeping-draughts. She never wakes up before eleven. I'll take care she has a good shut-eye on Monday night."

He chuckled softly, but he still wasn't satisfied.

"How about the housekeeper? What time does she arrive in the morning?"

"Not till eight o'clock."

"Okay."

He kept his eyes on the road ahead, but they were slits of concentration. He thought she hadn't done too badly. He couldn't have cased the joint better himself.

"That's my baby," he said. "Where will I find the sparklers?"

"In Mrs. Hull's bedroom." She said quietly: "The other side of Icklingham there's a lonely bit of road. You can pull up somewhere along it and we'll go over the layout."

After leaving Icklingham the terrain changed. Great undulating sandy bracken-covered stretches, with short spiky grasses and dotted with odd groups of pine trees. It looked wild, uncared for, isolated, only the road lying smooth and solid across this buff-coloured tract of country indicated the nearness of any human habitation.

About a mile along the road Patrick pulled into the verge close to a line of tall poplars. While he lit fresh cigarettes Myra took a folded piece of paper from her handbag and spread it out. She had made a rough pencil sketch of the ground floor plan of the house including the driveways and the outbuildings. She produced a propelling pencil from her bag and proceeded to explain the layout.

"At the end of this drive," she pointed with the pencil to the left of the house, "is the garage. As you can see it stands well back from the house. There's a workshop and store-shed here, and above it is the chauffeur's flat. But he won't be there when you come. Here, right at the back, is the kitchen, pantry and what-have-you, and adjoining this at the front of the house is a small study with a door opening on to the driveway at the side. Over the kitchen is the housekeeper's room. My room is here, on the front of the house over the study."

"Okay," he said through a mouthful of tobacco-smoke.

"Ground floor again," the pencil moved over the drawing. "Dining-room next to the study, then a wide hall with main staircase and drawing-room. Upstairs in front are the two guest-rooms with bathroom dividing them. Overlooking the back gardens is Hull's room, then comes another bathroom, Mrs. Hull's dressing-room and her bedroom at the end. As well as the door into her bedroom, the dressing-room has another entrance from the landing."

She glanced at him and he nodded his complete understanding of the layout. She really had done a good job on preparing the ground for him.

"Everywhere's carpeted," she was saying. "Not that Mrs. Hull is liable to wake, like I said before. Under Mrs. Hull's bedroom and dressing-room is the library. This door opens into the end of the hall. A few steps along you come to the main staircase. Here's another staircase outside the kitchen here, you see. But this is where you are, the main staircase, and on the landing, facing you, here, to your right, is the door of the bedroom."

"Which is where the sparklers are," he said.

Ten

She caught the look on his face and a momentary sickening sensation gripped her, but she pushed it aside. She moved the pencil again. "I'll come back to that in a moment," she said. She pointed to the two lines on the paper illustrating the driveway on the right of the house. "Just about here is a gravel-path that leads through a clump of shrubs and firs to the potting-shed, greenhouses and the walled garden. It's screened off from the house and the road. This path takes tradesmen's vans and anyone delivering stuff."

She broke off and stubbed out her cigarette. "Now Ted," she said. "You can't leave the car in the road. Not that anyone's likely to be about at that hour, but if it was seen standing outside it might arouse curiosity. So my advice is that you drive in and park it here, where it will be hidden from the house and the road. The gates will be open."

Patrick's arm around her shoulder pressed her to him, so that she looked at him, her mouth open a little, her eyes bright.

"You're right on the beam, hon," he said.

"From here," she went on, "you go round the side of the house to the french window of the library. I'll be waiting to let you in."

"Okay," he said. "Now let's get back to the bedroom. Will the door to her bedroom be locked?"

She shook her head.

"Where do I go for it? The stuff?"

"Beside the bed," she said. "A wall-safe."

It was a Chubb Size Five, a wall-safe, secured by special bolts and becoming an integral part of the very structure of the house. He recognized the type from Myra's detailed description. Of solid steel, with additional drill-resisting reinforcement over the entire area of the lockcase, the lock itself further protected by steel plate to a total thickness of seven-eighths of an inch. The door, fitted with three moving bolts of three-quarters of an inch in diameter was controlled by a three-wheel type keyless combination lock.

Then she told him what else she'd discovered about the combination, and he grinned at her first in disbelief, and then with delight. She reiterated what she'd told him, under his probing questions.

He was lighting a fresh cigarette for her, and she took a couple of drags at it.

"I can't tell you exactly all what's in it, but you can take it from me there'll be forty thousand pounds' worth of junk."

Patrick sat back relaxed, his fingers drumming on the steering-wheel. "Not bad junk, at that," he said.

He turned to her with a warm smile. "It's going to be like taking candy from a baby. With your co-operation I can be in and out of the dump in ten minutes. What time will it be okay for me to show up?"

"Give them a quarter-of-an-hour, Ted," Myra said thoughtfully. "They should leave before five-thirty, but if you make it a quarter-to-six—"

"I'm not likely to run across anybody, the postman or milkman at that hour?"

She shook her head emphatically.

"Post doesn't come till seven-thirty and the milkman's never there before eight. You shouldn't even see anyone on the road at that time. The farmhands don't start work until seven."

He smiled his satisfaction.

"So there's only one thing more to fix," he said. "Some pre-arranged signal between us just in case there's a slip-up."

She dropped the pencil back into her bag.

"I've thought of that," she said. "First thing when you get there take a look at my bedroom window, first floor left at the end. If anything's gone wrong, I'll keep the curtains closed. If they're open—"

"Proceed as arranged."

"But will it go wrong, Ted?" she said. "I mean what could? Short of accident or sudden illness in the house, Hull will be leaving at five-thirty or before."

"Relax, hon," he said. "Of course, nothing can go wrong."

"Oh, Ted," she said,.and she flung her arms round his neck and buried her face in his shoulder.

He was thinking of the car snatch which made it imperative that he had to pull off the caper at the time or not at all. Or, at least, delay it a few weeks. He said into her ear: "If your curtains are closed, I can perhaps hold everything for half-an-hour; but no more, I'll have to shove back to the smoke and you can phone me there. If it goes sour on us, we'll make a new plan."

She drew back her face to look at him, and he gave her a confident smile. "I know all this isn't going to be necessary," he told her. "It's just so we'll know what we're going to do whichever way the cat jumps."

She suddenly clutched his hand tightly, her face anxious. "Nothing must go wrong, Ted," she whispered. "This is your last job, Ted, for the sake of our future together."

He pulled her to him close, and then gently held her chin up to him.

"Relax on it, hon," he said. "We've planned this so perfect, you and me, nothing's going to stop us seeing it through. Nothing's going to take away that future together."

She relaxed and nestled closer to him.

"Ted, darling," she murmured. "We're going to be okay."

"Sure, we're going to be okay."

After giving her a few minutes close attention to take her mind off the project and to drive away any fears she might have, he broke it up by taking up the plan she'd sketched, which had slipped to the floor of the car.

"You won't need this, hon," he said. "I'd like to study it some more when I've taken a look at the house."

She nodded and sat up in the seat, straightening her hair.

"I meant you should keep it."

He slipped it in his pocket and started the engine.

"Better push on to Fowler's Inn," he grinned.

They got tea at the inn and afterwards drove leisurely on to the Suffolk-Norfolk border. They stopped for a drink at a little pub overlooking the Little Ouse, and then continued eastward to Thetford. They ate at the small hotel adjoining the cross-roads in the town and it was just after nine when they returned to Bury.

Patrick had agreed to Myra's suggestion that she should go back to Hickham by bus to avoid any chance of their being seen together unnecessarily, and he stopped the car again on Market Hill.

"It's a few minutes yet before my bus goes," she said. "We've thought of everything, haven't we?"

He nodded. He couldn't think of a single thing they'd missed out on.

"You got the phone number of my flat. Any change in our arrangement over the weekend, you phone me there before three Monday afternoon. I'll be starting my journey down about that time."

"I'll remember that," she said. "But there shouldn't be any need to phone. And if I see you in the morning in Hickham we'd better not recognize each other."

He was eyeing her with appreciation.

"You've certainly put your heart in this, hon," he said warmly. "You've done a great job of it."

"It's the last one, Ted, and our future's staked on it. That's why."

She leaned forward and kissed him. The passion in her embrace took his breath away. They clung together.

After a moment she drew back and opened the door of the car. "See you Tuesday morning," she said, then added in a whisper: "In the library."

He watched her walk quickly away through the parking lot towards the bus, trim-figured and a real eyeful to watch.

He saw the bus throb away, but he went on sitting in the car, smoking a cigarette, silently congratulating himself. He thought it had all worked out well.

The job was in the bag.

Eleven

Patrick stayed the night at the Angel Hotel. It was a typical Suffolk inn in the centre of the town with a mass of oak beams and dark panelling. The service was good, the room comfortable and there was a garage for the car. He spent the evening in the lounge-bar quietly drinking whisky and then went to bed. He spent an hour or so in bed poring over Myra's plan of the house, absorbing it in his mind so that he could memorize where everything was. Quite the little artist, Myra was, the way she had drawn the map, so that he had a clear view in his mind's eye of it. He slept well.

At nine-thirty next morning he left the Angel and drove to Hickham. He took the same route he had followed with Myra the previous afternoon.

He drove through the village and past the house. He saw no movement in the gardens and the quiet road was deserted. He drove on about a hundred yards and pulled up opposite a telephone-kiosk. It was a call-box Myra had said she used. Not too far from the house, but far enough to give her complete privacy. The kiosk was planted back from the road among some elder shrubs, which partially screened three sides of it.

He left the car and walked back along the road to the extensive frontage of the house. When he drew level with the open gates he paused and lit a cigarette. While he faked the reluctance of his lighter to operate, he studied the scene.

The house had recessed wooden-framed windows and a tall square-cut white porch surrounding the front door. His gaze focused on a small upstairs window. This was Myra's bedroom. The curtains were drawn aside. The way he hoped they would be when he looked there for the all-clear early on Tuesday morning.

Up the drive on the right he could just discern the junction of the gravel-path leading to the garden sheds. It was concealed on either side by trees and a shrubbery, and was an ideal place to park the car. He would drive up and reverse into it, he thought.

With his cigarette alight at last he walked on, past the next driveway where, through the open gates he had a good view of the side of the house. He could see the study door in the side of the wall and beyond it the kitchen windows. The gravel drive continued past these to the garage standing back from the corner of the house. There were outbuildings adjoining it and, as Myra had said, living accommodation above.

Patrick continued his walk to the bend in the road, and then retraced his steps, passing the house again without a pause. Then he went back to the car positive that he had seen no one either from the house or on the road. He didn't think there were any special features to note. He'd weighed up the place satisfactorily and with the help of Myra's artistic talent, he had a good picture of what he was tackling both inside and out. Myra was doing her stuff even more efficiently than he had hoped. He hadn't doubted that she would be there in the library waiting to let him in.

He started the car and drove back over a different route to Bury. He passed through the town to the south-east fringe and found the roundabout he had negotiated on his way the previous day. Instead of heading back along the route he had memorized the day before, he took the Ipswich road.

He used the throttle lightly. He had plenty of time. It was pushing ten-thirty. All he had to do was to fix the route in his mind and watch out for a likely place to dispose of the car he planned to knock off.

He had already decided on Ipswich as the point from which he would return to London by train. There, he would be travelling with a host of other passengers; inconspicuous, a stranger among a crowd. No one would notice him, or remember him. There would be nothing to connect him with the Hickham Hall operation, or with the stolen car when it was found. And to clinch it, there was his alibi.

On the other hand, he told himself, if he could rid himself of the car in some place where it wasn't found for a few days, a week or two even, so much the better. It would help him no end to get himself out of the country before the police had a chance to link the missing car from the *Spinning Wheel* off Eastern Avenue and the job seventy miles away at Hickham Hall.

He lit a cigarette and pondered the point. That was the trick. To dump the car where it wouldn't be found. It wasn't easy, or it would have been tried more often before.

Always when a stolen vehicle had been used for a snatch it was found abandoned soon afterwards. It wasn't any easy thing to hide even in the country. If he dumped it in a copse or found a disused barn or some other broken-down building, it was sure to be discovered in a few hours by a farm-worker, gamekeeper or some nosey character who would promptly yap their heads off. And the connecting link would be forged within an hour. He'd got to think of something better than that. He got himself no ideas at all from the terrain he passed through.

The road was well used, but it had got a good surface. He thought that even in the early morning it carried a fair load of traffic. Trucks, milk-lorries, odd cars. All around him ran gently undulating spaces, wooded and patterned with open fields of young green corn. Nothing that offered safe conceal-ment for any object as large as a car. Not that he was anxious to find a spot there and then. It was too far from Ipswich. He had to remember he had some walking to do, and he planned to get an early train.

The thought pushed him along a little faster. He'd need more time for study nearer his destination. There was no point in hanging back twenty miles away.

He was cruising at fifty when he approached Stowmarket. He slowed down to the speed-limit as he ran into the outskirts. He was careful about this. He couldn't afford to be pulled up for speeding. Though he'd seen no sign of the mobile police that morning.

There was nothing particularly outstanding about the place as he drove through the main street, and he took no more interest than what was necessary to note his route. Ipswich was twelve miles ahead and Needham Market was four. He thought he'd have to begin searching for a safe spot the other side of Stowmarket.

On the Ipswich side of Needham Market he pulled into a service station and got the tank filled. He was still searching for something he couldn't put into words so he made no inquiries about the district to the man who filled the tank. He drove out on to the road again telling himself that he had only another four or five miles in which to pick his spot. But there was noth-ing to suggest he'd find it along the main road.

Traffic was light and he idled up behind an open-back lorry

wondering if he should try one or other of the side roads, but before he could make a decision he found himself among some scattered cottages. It was a village called Blakenham. He kept behind the lorry through the village and was about to pull out and overtake, with the idea of turning off at the next road junction, when the large white lettering on the tail-board of the lorry registered for the first time on his mind. *Wenstone Quarries Ltd.* That was all, but it was enough to give him an idea.

The lorry was empty but the white daubs across the dark painted tailboard told him the stuff it carried. Chalk. There was sure to be old chalk-workings where the lorry was going to, and the chances were there would be water in them. That kind of grave would be the perfect solution.

He remained in line on the nearside, hanging back a little, following the bulky vehicle at a discreet distance, praying that the quarry was in the vicinity. He remained on the trail for another couple of miles. He began to think they were getting too near the town for a quarry-site and that the lorry might lead him miles the other side when the driver ahead thrust out his hand and turned right on to a narrow lane.

Patrick let him go and drove slowly past on the major road noting the white splashes on the tarmac of the lane. A few yards on he pulled into the side and looked back. The quarry wasn't far away. The lorries wouldn't have to run far before the chalk on their tyres was removed by their revolutions on the road.

The chalk-marks were still in evidence on the lane which suggested that the workings must be somewhere nearby, probably the other side of the shallow hill towards which the lane ran.

The road was clear and he turned the car round quickly, drove back and into the lane. It was narrow, less than the width of two cars, but there were frequent bays on either side where two lorries could have passed each other. As the road traversed the shallow incline towards the top of the hill it became flanked on either side with grass-covered banks, and elder shrubs, tangled bushes and stunted firs blanketing the view of the fields.

Topping the rise he slowed the car and drove cautiously round the long twists the road made through the banks of vegetation. There was a sudden dip ahead and the road straightened for about fifty yards and through a thin screen of bush on his left he saw the drop and across it the darkly scarred walls of white chalk.

He pulled up and reversed back to the first available bay. The road was deserted, but he could hear the faint working of the mechanical grab in the distance. He walked back to the spot he had noticed from the car and peered through the bush.

The edge of the quarry was a few feet away, a margin of grass-covered ground separated the drop from the road. He could not see how deep it was at this point, but looking across the great opening the mechanical diggers and grabs had made into the shallow hillside it was evident that the quarry was deep. All the activity was going on on the further side, nearly a quarter of a mile away.

The area nearest him was now no longer used, and between it and the new workings mounds of earth and chalk had pushed up, scattered with vegetation and encircling water-filled pockets of various depths. He could see above a high mound the gantry of a digger and hear its engine throbbing, and further away stood a couple of waiting lorries.

At the end of a built-up track on the further side he saw a green-painted wooden office building with a white asbestos roof.

He moved a few yards further down the road to a place where the bank levelled out. There was a gap here that had once been the gateway into a field. It was uneven and covered in parts with spreading bramble bushes, but it was wide enough to get a car through without leaving much evidence of the operation. He stepped through it after ensuring he was hidden from the workmen by the jutting wall of the quarry which curved round to form a basin of the greater part of the old workings.

He moved to the edge and looked down.

It was a sheer drop of some forty feet into brackenishblue water. He couldn't estimate the depth but he decided it was sufficient to cover up a car. It was the kind of place he'd dreamed about for the job, but had never dared hope to find.

He made his way back to the car and drove down the gently descending lane to find the limits of the quarry extended to the edge of another road. This skirted the depression, passing the entrance to the present workings where the office was situated.

He turned the car round slowly, noting the lie of the land. There was a farmhouse in the distance on another rise and a pair of cottages near the road. Apart from these the surroundings were isolated.

He turned back into the lane and up the hill, his eyes raking the gateway again as he went slowly past. He began to work out the timing. He'd have to get here from Hickham and dump the car before seven on Tuesday morning. He reckoned the quarrymen started work at seven; but if it was later he couldn't risk arriving after that himself. Farmworkers were early birds, and he might be seen.

He noted the arable land close by, which even to his city eyes indicated that there might be workers in the fields. And dropping a car that depth would create one hell of a splash. He had to get the disposal over before seven for that reason. Then there was the walk into Ipswich. He might get a lift, but that was risky. He'd prefer to walk if there was time. But he reckoned on catching an early train.

He came out of the lane, back on to the major road and turned right. He travelled slowly but soon found himself at a road junction. He followed the finger-post which indicated two miles to Ipswich and a few minutes later came up with the outskirts of the town. He noted the bus terminus, and decided he'd have no more than a three mile walk which he reckoned he could do in under the hour.

He drove into the centre of the town and at the car-park inquired the way to the station. He went down the short hill of Lloyds Avenue. The traffic lights were green. He crossed the intersection in front of the town hall and along Princes Street, passed offices and shops and motor and agricultural engineering showrooms and found the railway-station car-park over the narrow river at the end.

He went in and bought a time-table and then sat in the car to look up the service. There was a train at seven-fifty-five. That would get him in town at nine-forty-three. That was the one.

He lit a cigarette and let the exhilaration of success flow through him.

The whole set-up was tailor-made. Everything worked out with machine-like precision. Both ends of the job were organized and he could relax for the weekend. He could enjoy an easy drive back to London. He glanced at his watch. It was a few minutes after twelve.

He started the car and drove back into the town to find a drink.

Twelve

The saturday afternoon sun had not much strength; but it was shining. Its diffused light gleamed on the long mustard-yellow bonnet of the rakish convertible Riviera phaeton as the three hundred and twenty h.p. supercharged engine of the 1934 Duesenberg droned along the A.11 at a rock-steady seventy-five.

Miss Frayle was glad that the hazy sunshine had not tempted Dr. Morelle into lowering the hood, since the March air was no comfort in an open car travelling at such speed. Even with the drop head up and the windows raised it was not possible to avoid the scurries of draught that seeped in through the joints where the hood frame fitted the windshield and side windows. But Miss Frayle had travelled far and often enough with Dr. Morelle to know the futility of making any complaint.

They had left Harley Street soon after eleven that morning, and had driven into Hertfordshire, taking the A. I. through Hatfield, Welwyn and Stevenage. Lunch at Baldock, and then via Royston on to the A.11., and the approaches to Newmarket.

Dr. Morelle was expected at four o'clock. Miss Frayle considered whimsically that if he did not treat the accelerator more lightly they would arrive considerably before the appointed time, apart from the fact that the speed at which he drove did not give her an opportunity to appreciate the surrounding scenery. Not that that was anything unusual. But the journey had come as a surprise.

The invitation to Clive Manor, at Lycham St. Marks, had been a long-standing one. Dr. Morelle had been too busy with work and travelling abroad to do more than vaguely promise Lady Carslake that he hoped to work it in during the summer. The previous summer, Miss Frayle was reflecting. The time had hurried by and all thought of the invitation had been lost in the pressure of work that had kept Dr. Morelle and herself fully occupied all winter in London. And then yesterday, they had suddenly been reminded of it.

Lady Carslake had telephoned and renewed her invitation with some urgency. She knew Dr. Morelle well enough to know that the surest way of enlisting his co-operation was to be candid. She had organized a charity bazaar in the village hall for that evening. Side-shows and stalls.

She had originally arranged for a television-star who was famous for his portrayal of Dr. Morelle in a series of television-films based on Dr. Morelle's cases which had been suitably fictionized, to open the bazaar and to judge the performance of the local amateur dramatic society in the play. "The blessed creature's let me down at the very last minute," she said. Would he himself, she begged Dr. Morelle, and his charming secretary, step into the breach? Could he help her out? She had gone on hurriedly to remind him of the long-standing invitation; to apologize for such impolite short notice; but she was desperate.

Dr. Morelle had been unable to refuse such an appeal and since his investigating committee had been set up and was ready to begin work the following Tuesday, allowing for a week-end free of both engagements and desk-work he had agreed, to Lady Carslake's delight, to drive down to Clive Manor.

Miss Frayle had met Lady Carslake on previous occasions. She had found her a charming middle-aged woman, who had devoted much of her time and energy to charity since the death of her husband, who had been on friendly terms with Dr. Morelle, as a result of their meeting in China in pre-war days, where Carslake had held a government post. Dr. Morelle had helped him out of some tricky situation, Miss Frayle rather believed. She was looking forward to seeing Clive Manor, and even the prospect of attending the village charity show filled her with mild curiosity and amusement. Stealing a glance at Dr. Morelle's gaunt, enigmatic profile, she wondered if he was anticipating the trip in a similar mood. She doubted it, he did not enjoy the simple pleasures of life. In fact, what did he enjoy?

At the junction where the Cambridge road joined the A.11, Dr. Morelle slowed the car to fall in with a short convoy of lorries. After a while he pulled out and the Duesenberg purred along the centre lane, overtaking the line of vehicles, and running into the outskirts of Newmarket at a more leisurely pace.

The wide road narrowed a little and became the spacious main street of the town and they drove slowly through it. Miss Frayle had been through Newmarket before, though that was some years ago, and all she could remember about it was its cleanliness and air of prosperity. It looked just the same to her now, bustling with people and motor traffic. There was little that was old or placid about the place, like some of the villages they had passed through. Most of the buildings lining the street were modern and many of the shops looked spacious. It had no doubt once been a thriving market-town, but now its most important industry was horse-racing and Miss Frayle was intrigued at the thought that the prosperity of a town could depend so much on race horses.

Round the clock-tower island at the end of the main thoroughfare, and the throbbing engine of the Duesenberg began to pick up the revs again as Dr. Morelle took it up through the gears. He eased into top and let the car coast for a moment along the wide tree-lined road.

"Have you studied the map?" Dr. Morelle said. "We turn off the A.11 at the intersection ahead, do we not?"

Miss Frayle pulled the map from the shelf beneath the deep facia board, turned it over on her knee and soon found their position.

"Yes, Dr. Morelle, that's right. You take the right fork, the A.45. This road goes on to Thetford."

Dr. Morelle nodded silently, glancing in the mirror before pulling across on to the right fork. Gently he began putting pressure on the accelerator again.

"Kentford isn't very far along," Miss Frayle said, her eyes on the map. "We turn off left there, and then—" She broke off, peering at the faint collection of lines denoting the Suffolk lanes. "There seem to be one or two routes to Lycham St. Marks. I don't know which road would be the best. It doesn't tell—"

"It isn't likely to be so confusing as it sounds," he interrupted her; a faint, fleeting smile of tolerance moved across his lips. "No doubt it will be signposted, and if there is any difficulty we should be able to inquire the way."

"Oh, yes, of course we can," she said. She had once admitted to him how much she disliked having to ask strangers to direct her, when she had lost her way. He had explained to her at some length the psychological motivations for her shyness. But she still avoided asking people the way if she could.

Miss Frayle pressed herself back in the seat, her eyes blinking behind her glasses first at the speedometer needle and then at the hedgerows flashing by as they sped along the last stretch of straight road leading to the village.

But the cross country route from Kentford proved to be easier to follow than she had anticipated. The roads were narrow but each turning was signposted. Through breaks in the roadside hedges she could see a pattern of grazing meadows and dark woods of fir with here and there a glimpse of a distant cottage. It was a strange terrain, she thought; part arable, part wild heath, part wooded; but there was a melancholy fascination about it that attracted her.

Dr. Morelle stopped the car at a signpost which indicated that they had reached Lycham St. Marks and Miss Frayle managed to whip her courage up sufficiently to inquire the way to Clive Manor from a passing farm-worker. They were nearer than they thought. The house was not more than half a mile along the road. They drove on, down a shallow incline through a narrow wooded valley and topping the rise on the other side saw the church spire of Lycham village above the trees away to their right.

On the left, a low stone wall fringed the grass verge, overshadowed by a privet hedge, and beyond this were firs and chestnut trees adequately spaced in well tended parkland. The entrance to the house formed a bay off the road. The tall iron gates were open, and as they drove through Miss Frayle noticed that the porter's lodge, a low single-storey building, was well-preserved although it appeared to be deserted. The drive curved through the park between two rows of trees which were linked by carefully-trimmed beds of shrubs and close-cropped grass. It ended in a spacious gravel crescent and Dr. Morelle brought the Duesenberg to a halt in front of the steps of the main porch.

It was a magnificent house and its well preserved appearance did not disguise its origins. Great mullion windows with turreted bays reached up to the eaves of the shallow sloping roof of faded red tiles. Between the ground and first floor windows the walls were richly decorated with pargeting. At one end was a narrow circular tower, topped by a lantern with a weather vane protruding from the apex of its cone roof. The double front doors were of massive oak set in a deep porch supported on pillars to which a short flight of steps led up.

As Miss Frayle and Dr. Morelle eyed the house the front doors opened and a manservant came down the steps, to open the car door, and a few moments later Miss Frayle, followed by Dr. Morelle stood in the great hall panelled from floor to lofty ceiling with dark oak, the walls richly carved and decorated at intervals with ancient armour. A wide oak staircase led up from the centre of the hall to a landing from which a short flight branched either way to a gallery running across the hall which led off into each wing of the house. At the head of the central landing was a huge portrait in oils of one of the late Sir Aubrey Carslake's ancestors, who had been a pioneer of the East India Company.

Lady Carslake appeared through a curtained Norman archway to the left of the stairs and hurried towards them.

"So delighted to have you here at last, Dr. Morelle," she said. "And I appreciate your kindness in making do with such short notice when I know how busy you are, but this charity show has just forced my hand. Anyway," and she smiled, "it's been responsible for getting you and Miss Frayle down here."

"I need no reason to bring me here other than the pleasure it gives me to accept the invitation," Dr. Morelle said. "I'm sorry to have been so long about it."

Miss Frayle sat down, looking out into the garden. It was beautifully laid out with terraces stretching down to wide close-cropped lawns and flowerbeds. At the end was a rockery with a small ornamental lake in the centre of which was a delicately carved figure. No doubt a fountain played from its upraised arm during the summer, Miss Frayle thought. The rock garden and the lake were sheltered by a ring of trimmed young firs. The limits of the gardens were marked by rhododendron shrubs and a neat hedge wall just behind them. Beyond this was parkland melting away to the boundary of the estate

Miss Frayle hoped the weather would remain fine for the side-shows at the village-hall, about which Lady Carslake was telling her and Dr. Morelle. She hoped too that there would be a fortune-teller.

Thirteen

A large, fleshy woman, expensively clothed and overdressed with jewellery came in, to be introduced as Mrs. Hull, who was helping with the bazaar. She at once appeared to be much taken up with Dr. Morelle, listening attentively to what he was saying with an expression of awe. No doubt, Miss Frayle thought, Lady Carslake had previously explained to her friend just how distinguished was the visitor from London, a thought from which Miss Frayle derived a certain proud satisfaction.

Tea came in on a silver trolley and while they sipped from delicate cups of bone china Lady Carslake went on about the bazaar and the charity for which it was organized. It was for an orphanage located in the district. A bazaar in the village hall at Lycham St. Marks was held each year from which one could always reckon to raise a good sun of money. Last year they had had a record total of one hundred and eighty-five pounds. This year, Lady Marsden hoped to do even better. They had a number of good stalls and side-shows, the play at the end of the programme, and she added, to Dr. Morelle's amusement, a distinguished psychiatrist and criminologist to open the proceedings and judge the talents of the local amateur society.

Miss Frayle made a few notes about the charity and the orphanage for Dr. Morelle to refer to at the opening and then the manservant reappeared to announce that the car was waiting, at the same reminding Lady Carslake that he was running a stall and was anxious to be in attendance before the customers appeared. Dr. Morelle and Mrs. Hull, followed by Lady Carslake and Miss Frayle went out to a luxurious limousine with a peak-capped driver at the wheel, which within ten minutes deposited them outside the village hall.

Inside the long, wooden, gaily decorated building was all the activity of a sale room before the customers arrived. Groups of people were putting the finishing touches to the small stage at the end of the room, and to the variety of stalls around the sides of the hall. Miss Frayle was surprised to see such a large collection of attractions and so many ingenious ways of persuading customers to part from their money. Stalls with hoop-la, rolling-the-penny, bottle tombola, Lotto, darts and a lucky-dip for the children. Produce stalls, run by efficient-look-ing village women, offered home-made cakes, pastries and sweets, bottled fruit and home-made jams and honey.

Along one side was a board with the announcement: *Bowling for the Pig,* nearby was the *Gold Mine.* This was a large flat box of turf, and contestants bought small pegs and staked their claims for the hidden golden sovereign that was the prize. The competitor's name was written on the peg and it was stuck in the turf in the place where the sovereign might be. This stall was operated by a thin elderly woman who was wearing an anx-ious expression, and Miss Frayle saw her constantly glance in Lady Carslake's direction as she and Mrs. Hull talked to one of the other women helpers who was running the refreshment stall.

Miss Frayle had just excitedly noticed the fortune-teller's sign, when the thin, harrassed-looking woman crossed to Lady Carslake. "The sovereign is missing," Miss Frayle heard her say. "I've been looking all over. I'm sure I had it with me when I came in. I was going to get my son to place it. But I can't find it anywhere."

"Oh, dear," Lady Carslake said anxiously. "I haven't an-other."

"Don't worry," Mrs. Hull said. "I've got two or three at home. I'll have one brought over."

Lady Carslake looked as grateful as the stall-holder. "Shall I send over to Hickham?" she said.

"No," Mrs. Hull smiled. "I'll telephone my maid. She knows where they are, and will come over in my car. She can be here with it inside fifteen minutes." Mrs. Hull went out to telephone from the front of the hall, and Lady Carslake turned to the women running the stall, while Miss Frayle's eyes brightened as she spotted the inevitable fortune-teller's tent which was an alcove discreetly enclosed with long red curtains.

She saw Dr. Morelle in conversation with two people near the stage, and Lady Carslake moving towards him. The two men on the door who took the money were getting ready to open up. Miss Frayle thought she would take the opportunity of visit-ing the fortune-teller before the hall became crowded and there was a queue.

No one appeared to notice her. She quickly covered the last few paces and opened the curtain.

The woman inside was fixing on a long, flowing headdress. She wore a voluminous shawl of many colours which almost hid the top of a black dress. She was thin, her face sharp-featured, her skin dry and the colour of mahogany. Her eyes were large and black. She wore large gold earrings and thick gold bangles enwrapped her wrists. She sat before a small table covered with black velvet, the centre bare except for the small crystal ball. The woman suddenly looked up and straight into Miss Frayle's eyes.

Miss Frayle wondered if she was a real gipsy living locally, brought in specially to run the fortune-teller's tent. At the thought she could feel her heart beat more quickly.

"I know the show hasn't quite opened yet," Miss Frayle said hesitantly, "but I thought I'd make a start before the crowd came."

"Come along in, my dear," the woman invited. "You're one of the helpers, I can see."

"No, not really. I'm a friend of Lady Carslake. I—"

"Please sit down, my dear."

Obediently Miss Frayle sat opposite her, the crystal between them. Suddenly the dark woman held out her hand, palm upward.

"Cross my palm with silver, my dear, before we can begin."

Miss Frayle found a half-crown from her handbag and placed it on the other's somewhat grimy palm. Miss Frayle felt sure she was a genuine gipsy as she slipped the coin away in a pocket of her dress.

"Your palm, the left hand."

Miss Frayle held out her open hand. The woman stared at it, then gazed into the crystal. After a little while she raised her eyes and there was a fixed stare in them.

"You do not live in these parts," she said quietly. "You live and work in a large city. London, perhaps?"

Miss Frayle nodded. "But you travel a good deal, abroad, in your employment, which you find very interesting work. You have and will continue to have good health, and no financial worries." The black eyes slowly lowered to the crystal again. "There is a man, tall and dark, some years older than you, who has a great influence on your life. You admire and respect him."

Miss Frayle felt herself blushing furiously, while at the same time she goggled at the woman, impressed by her accuracy. Her description certainly fitted Dr. Morelle. She waited expectantly, staring at the crystal, which seemed to glow, and then at the woman's face.

"You are involved in some experiment," the woman was continuing, "something concerned with your job. Something quite unusual, but I can see it is going to be a success."

She closed her eyes for a moment and then opening them wide, Miss Frayle wondered what was coming next.

"I see a figure, a fair figure, someone from the past. It is not a friend or acquaintance. Just someone you have seen and who is important in some way to you. And you will see this person again in the very near future. There is another man, too, far in the background. A young man. But I cannot see much about him. It is too far in the future." She moved her head closer to the crystal. "Now the picture grows dim. The future fades." She looked up and smiled a conspiratorial smile. "But it is bright with happiness for you."

Thanking her, Miss Frayle went out of the tent into the hall, surprised to find it already noisy and crowded. The doors were open and people were flooding in, the stallholders were already inviting customers to try their skill.

Lady Carslake and Dr. Morelle, she saw, were up on the stage ready for the formal opening. Miss Frayle turned to see Mrs. Hull move towards the doors, and at that moment a girl came in and looked around her. Mrs. Hull saw her and they met just inside the hall. Miss Frayle guessed that it was the maidservant who had brought the sovereign.

After a few moments, the girl turned and started to walk out.

Miss Frayle suddenly remembered what the gipsy woman had just told her. Someone she had seen in the past. This was the someone. This girl. She felt certain she knew the face, the blonde hair. Where had she seen her before? Who was she? And why should she remember her?

The girl had gone but the picture of her remained to taunt Miss Frayle's memory. The fortune-teller had foretold that some girl would come into her life out of the past. And she knew she had seen the girl before.

Miss Frayle did not know where, or how, or why she should think it important. Maybe it would come to her if she stopped trying to remember. She realized she was frowning to herself, as if something had disquieted her. Something the gipsy woman had told her. The blonde young woman. She told herself she was being silly, and she determined not to let the dark thought which had invaded her mind prevent her enjoying herself. She had decided to have a go at everything. But first she would hear what Dr. Morelle had to say.

She edged her way through the crowd nearer the stage as Lady Carslake stepped to the front of the platform.

Fourteen

Harry Price turned out of Oakley Street, where his current girl-friend had a top-floor back room, strolled along the King's Road in the direction of Sloane Square. Dusk had fallen as he casually made his way along the pavement, a continuing pattern of shadow alternating with shafts of light from the shop-windows.

Price knew this part of London well. It is not very wide, the King's Road. It starts just beyond Buckinham Palace and runs through Eaton Square, now transformed into elegant flats; it narrows at Sloane Square and continues past the Duke of York's Barracks, with its sports-field and cinder-track, where star athletes may be seen training.

Harry Price passed the pubs on either pavement, the restaurants, the coffee-bars, the cinema where they showed foreign films, the town hall, the eighteenth-century houses, the roomy or the squalid studios, the antique dealers. Behind him lay that end of the King's Road which made a dangerous turn to the left and the right to finish at the pub they called World's End.

Not that Price was thinking about all this. He was thinking, about the girl in the top-floor back. She was a little film-extra, pert and pretty, and he'd spun her the usual line about helping her with her career. He wasn't thinking about it at all then, but he knew that whenever a news-story broke about a murder, a lovers' death-pact, a suicide, a bankruptcy, an eccentric all-night party, nine times out of ten it had originated in this part of the world.

He had watched the King's Road restaurants and coffee-bars start up, places decorated with indoor plants and run by lovely girls posing as Mediterranean peasants, or by handsome youths in jeans, open-necked shirts, and he had noted the innumerable restaurants opening up with Indian food, Greek food, Italian food. Sometimes there was guitar-music to remind the customers of holidays spent in sunny Spain.

He knew the King's Road on a Saturday morning, not too early. It doesn't start early. Nothing starts early in the morning in the King's Road. He knew the faces in the off-licences, in the cafés, in the picture-framers, in the coffee-bars, in the pubs and drinking-clubs after half past eleven. Writers and editors, actors and artists; and Harry Price knew the con-men and the grifters who operated from this part of the world, sometimes marked down their prey in the pubs in the King's Road. The way Neville Heath had done, and George Haigh; and a few other cheap crooks who'd turned to murder in the end.

And Price had been around, gate-crashed or otherwise, the parties in the studios, in the bare attics, in the damp, frowsty basement bed-sitters. He knew the midnight oil was burnt not only in revelry. Sometimes the blackmail letters were written; the compromising photographs were taken. The latest swindle was worked out in the midnight hours, the latest gambling racket planned.

And in the pubs and coffee-bars he could overhear the Tweedy Set talking loudly about "Buck House", or he could note the wide boys, work-shy and shifty-eyed, planning a dog-track coup; or artists panning their pals with the acid vehemence some creative people use towards other creative people. He knew the bold faces of the smooth young men who gate-crash parties with tight trousers and a bland assurance, their eyes sharp for the handbag left lying about uncared for.

He knew the King's Road as it was twenty-four hours in the day. Its ambitions and its pleasures, its vice, its beauty. Its crime.

That was the King's Road as he'd known it, all the years he'd lived there. And though he'd moved away, because he'd somehow reasoned that he himself had become too well-known around there, and that wasn't a good thing, he still liked it best of all as a place to live. He thought he might go back there, some day.

Arrived at Sloane Square, Harry Price bought his ticket and went down into the tube station. And now he wasn't even thinking about the current girl-friend. His thoughts were leaning forward, focusing themselves on the meeting ahead with Ted Patrick, and the caper that was being lined up for him.

He gave an involuntary shiver for no reason at all that he could think of, and he put it down to the draught blowing up the stairs from the blackness of the tunnel below.

When the telephone rang Ted Patrick was enjoying a

scotch and soda and awaiting the arrival of Harry Price.

It was Monday evening and everything was set and he was ready to go. The unexpected burr-burr of the phone upset his buoyant mood. Price ringing to say he'd changed his mind?

Price had been even more anxious to do the job when Patrick had called on him the previous evening to confirm the details. But now that the fulfilment of his plans was imminent, Patrick dreaded the sudden thought that something was turning up to stall him.

He grabbed the receiver and his relief to find it wasn't Price turned to alarm when he heard Myra's voice over the wire. She heard the note in his tone.

"It's okay, Ted, nothing's changed," she said quickly. "But I had to let you know I won't be in the house tomorrow morning. Got to go over with Hull to Newmarket."

"You got to go where?" He was so concerned that her news meant the whole caper was off he didn't at first catch the drift of what she was saying.

"Newmarket," she was saying. "He asked me to go with him. Listen, Ted, I'm talking from the call-box, you know, and I got to make it snappy, so I won't go into details. But you got nothing to worry about. We're leaving at half past five in the morning. To-morrow morning. I can't do anything about it; but it doesn't make any difference. You don't really need me there, and everything will still be as arranged for you."

He gave a sigh and relaxed. No, he didn't need her there, provided she left the all-clear signal and the french window unlocked. It was okay by him if she had to go. Maybe it would turn out easier that way. She might fuss or panic at the last minute if she was with him.

"You had me worried there for a bit, hon." His confidence welled up inside him again and oozed into his voice, "Thought everything had gone up the spout when I heard you on the line. But you go ahead. I know what to do and where to find everything."

"I knew you'd be okay, Ted," she said.

He gave a little laugh.

"Put over a convincing act," he said. "And allow a safe margin of time. Then get in touch."

"My thoughts will be with you," Myra said. "Good luck, Ted."

"Be seeing you." He hung up and stared at the receiver. So he was going it all alone. He couldn't get in touch with her again before the job.

It occurred to him that he hadn't repeated their arrangements in detail for confirmation. He ought to have done that. Only she hadn't said anything about it. She had obviously taken them as set, since nothing had come up to change them, and she had been wise to keep the chat to the minimum over the phone. That had been his own automatic reaction. It needed no more than a crossed line, an overheard word or two, to set suspicion working in some chance eavesdropper's nasty mind.

He finished his drink and a few minutes later Price arrived.

Harry Price wore the same clothes he'd had on when Patrick had first visited him, but the shirt had been washed. He'd shaved and his hair was groomed. He was all ready and eager for the part. Patrick had laid out the clothes on the divan-bed and now he pushed aside the dividing curtain and brought them out into the living-room.

"Get into these first." He handed the other a light tweed jacket, and a pullover. "And here's the tie I usually wear."

"Looks like being a nice fit," Price grinned, appraising the clothes as he put them over his arm. "Nice bit of tweed."

He crossed into the bedroom and began to change. While he did so Patrick removed the whisky-bottle from the table and put it in the sideboard cupboard next to a half-bottle of gin. He closed the door and went into the kitchen to get his old raincoat and soft hat.

He put the coat and hat over a chair and went into the bedroom as Price finished dressing. Patrick produced an eyebrow pencil, and they returned to the living-room after Price had studied his reflection in the mirror.

"Just darken the eyebrows a bit," Patrick said, pushing Price into a chair. He got to work with the pencil, then stood back surveying his work. "That should do nicely," he said. "Try the hat and coat."

Price did so, pulling the brim of the hat down over his left eye.

"Stand over there," Patrick said. He nodded. "You'll do."

78

Price peeled off the coat and dropped the hat on top of it. He sat down. "It calls for a little drink, eh?"

"You'll be calling at one or two pubs to-night," Patrick said. "Better go easy on the booze." But he went to the sideboard and came back with two small whiskies. He mixed plenty of water with the one he handed to Price.

"For the next twenty-four hours you're Ted Patrick," he said. "Don't forget it. Don't overdo it. And remember, I'm a moderate drinker."

Price raised his glass, his lips already curling to take it.

"I never had a better part," he said. "Here's success to my performance." He swallowed half the drink at a gulp. "Now, what's the routine exactly?"

Patrick told him it wasn't a pub-crawl. There were just three spots he occasionally visited in the evening, and he wrote down their names, together with the names of the barmaids and barmen. Price was to stay in the background and linger over no more than a couple of drinks at each pub.

"Keep away from the bar when you've got your drinks," he went on. "No one'll take any notice. I usually stay on my own and I never try to horse around or gag with the barmaids. It'll just look as if I've been seen at each place."

"What about any regulars you might know?" Price said.

"I haven't been regular enough to get friendly," Patrick said. "If it does get to look like a party, finish your drink and get out." He took a card out of his wallet. "I haven't been to this clip-joint in months. It might be an idea to look in there to round off the night." He handed Price the card. "That'll get you in."

"What do I do there?"

"Just sit around with a drink and watch the floor-show." Patrick wrote down the names of the door-keeper and a couple of the waiters. "They'll have practically forgotten what I look like, but don't give them a chance to look too closely."

Price said with a grin: "What's the floor-show like?"

"The usual stuff. I don't go in for that stuff. You keep away and have a quiet drink. Just so you're seen."

"Watching the girls suits me," Price said affably. "What time d'you want me to leave?"

"Get a taxi back here in the early hours."

He threw a key on to the table. "Give the driver the impression you've had a few. Make a bit of play with the key there, opening the door. So that he'll remember the scene."

Price nodded and drained his glass.

"I get it," he said.

Patrick left the flat just before three that afternoon. He was satisfied that Price wouldn't fluff his part and they'd had one final run-through of the routine over sandwiches and coffee. Price knew he had to keep quiet and stay away from the windows for the rest of the afternoon. All he had to do was to wait around the flat till darkness, and start his performance at eight o'clock.

Fifteen

Patrick walked through to Praed Street and got the Metropolitan to Liverpool Street. He changed to the Central and waited for a Hainault train.

Half-an-hour later he was up in the fresh air again, on Eastern Avenue. It was a few minutes after four when he came out of Gant's Hill Station. He had a lot of time to lose. He crossed the road to the cinema and lost some of it there. He got a seat right at the back of the half-empty cinema and didn't follow the programme very attentively. He watched the first few minutes of film and dropped off to sleep. He woke up in the middle of the second feature, and strolled out into the night.

He joined a couple at the bus stop and by seven-thirty he was trundling along towards the *Spinning Wheel* in a double-decker. It was a stop and start jaunt but he had timed it nicely.

Where the bus turned off Eastern Avenue he hopped out and the walk to the roundabout took him ten minutes. The wind was cold and threw spatters of rain in his face. He turned up the collar of his new navy burberry and tugged his dark hat a little lower over his eyes. He glanced across at the service station. The showroom lights were out, but the place was still open for business.

He turned off and walked briskly towards the floodlit roadhouse.

The car-park was already well-packed, with cars still arriving. Some came up from Eastern Avenue, others from the other direction. Patrick looked for the car-park attendant first. There was a light on in his hut and the door was half-open. He could see the uniformed figure directing a flashy car in at the other end of the block.

There was a van parked on the edge of the park nearest him and he slipped up beside it, watching the scene, hidden from the man. Cars were still coming in, but mostly they made the entrance the other end nearest the house and where the man was.

While he stood there sizing up the situation a car swung into the centre gap in the chain and pulled up in a vacant space in the last row of cars, nearest the road, a few yards from him.

He had been beside the van not more than a minute, and he now moved away and walked along between the second and third row of cars, heading towards the house entrance as if he had just parked his car. As he went by the new arrival in the third row he studied the car and the occupants who were just getting out.

It was a Vauxhall, similar to the model he had hired when he had driven down on Friday. He made a mental note of the number. Two girls and a man stood waiting for the driver and talking loudly as he locked the door.

Patrick moved on slowly until he had the floodlit entrance close enough, then he stopped and lit a cigarette. The foursome passed him and he noted their faces in the lights. He let them get inside and then, puffing at his cigarette, he made for the entrance, too.

The two girls had obviously gone straight upstairs to the powder room. Patrick saw the two men go into the cocktail lounge as he got into the hall. He thought that they looked as if they were out to make a night of it. That meant they'd be there until the early hours.

He went into the saloon. It was well patronized with groups of people clustered around the bar. Many of the tables were occupied, but he found a vacant one near the door. He dropped his hat and coat on a chair, pushed through the crowd and bought himself a double whisky. He went back to the table and sat down.

After a while he left his drink and coat and went out giving the impression he was looking for the lavatory. He found the place through a door to the right and along a passage adjoining the end of the saloon.

He wasn't gone many moments and when he returned to the hall, he went into the cocktail lounge.

He could hear the dance-band, and through the archway he could see the customers taking their places for dinner and beyond the dining-room, couples were leaving the tables at the side and going on to the floor.

There was no sign of his pretty waitress. There were a dozen people in the lounge, so busy talking they didn't notice him. As he went towards the little bar in the corner, the foursome he'd been trailing passed through into the dining-room and followed the waiter to a table.

He bought a single whisky and drank it slowly while he watched the foursome settle down and start to order. He finished his drink and went back into the saloon. He sat down, and lit a cigarette.

It was eight-fifteen. The garage closed at eight-thirty. He gave himself another five minutes, then he drained his glass and went out, putting his coat and hat on in the hall.

At the door, he turned quickly away to the right and up the road. It was quite dark away from the front of the building. He continued up the road a few yards. Then he came back. The car-park attendant was engrossed in a book or some paper work inside his hut.

Patrick could see the lights of the cars passing along Eastern Avenue, and the pump lights glowing at the garage. But he moved in shadow. There was no one on the road and for the moment the car park was dead. He slipped in through the centre gap and up alongside the Vauxhall.

He knew the car was locked, but he tried the button release automatically. The button gave to his pressure, but the catch stayed fixed.

It was a matter of seconds to slip the strong flexible wire from the deep pocket of his burberry, bend one end into a hook and bend it again half way so that the distance between the hook and the angle was about the depth of the driving-window of the car. He wedged the wire in his armpit and placed his palms on the window, pressing the glass downward.

Gradually it moved until there was a gap of about a quarter-inch between the frame at the top. He quickly slipped the wire over and down inside, manoeuvring the hook round the swivel catch of the ventilating window. A tug and it swivelled down, releasing the arm-lock. Pressure on the front end brought the small triangular ventilator pivoting round and he slipped his hand in and drew back the lock of the door.

The car-park was still quiet. The attendant out of the way in his hut.

Patrick opened the door, pushed the wire in his pocket and took out his pencil torch. Leaning low inside, close to the instrument-panel, he switched on and read the number of the ignition lock.

It was an FA series.

He memorized the three figures, closed the door and moved away into the road.

The faint shower of rain had stopped but the clouds were massing up, blotting out the cold stars. The wind had dropped and the night had all the appearance of an imminent storm. It was pushing eight-thirty when he reached the end of the road. He paused, looking across at the garage.

As he stood there the pump lights went out, then the outside lamps were switched off.

Eastern Avenue had quietened a bit and Patrick moved off across the road. When he went up the drive-in the office light went out and he saw a figure at the door and could hear the rattle of keys.

He quickened his pace.

"Hope I'm not too late," he said as he came up with the attendant. "But I'm in a bit of a fix. Gone and left my keys in my car and slammed the door."

The man looked round as if searching for the car. It was too dark for him to see Patrick's face, the collar was turned up and the hat brim low.

Patrick pointed casually over his shoulder.

"Up at the *Spinning Wheel,*" he said lightly. "Took in a party. Mind wasn't on the job. Slammed the door with the keys in. Just realized it, and thought you'd probably have one."

"Oh, yes, sir, we have them," The man was satisfied. He began to open the office door again. "What model is it?"

"Vauxhall. I can give you the number."

The man went in, switched on the light and went behind the short counter and began to sort through bunches of keys. Patrick remained at the door and faked a coughing fit, practically hiding his face in a handkerchief. The man came back with a key. Patrick remained outside in the shadows, clearing his throat.

"That's the one, sir."

Patrick took the key and gave the man half-a-crown.

"Have a drink on me."

Patrick walked away, waving aside the man's thanks, and he was back on the other side of the road by the time the office light went out again.

As he returned to the roadhouse he heard a motor-cycle roar into life, and saw the man from the garage swing on to Eastern Avenue and streak away.

The car-park was quiet. The faint strains of dance-music seeped out from the building. As he went by on the opposite side of the road a couple appeared in the entrance and went towards one of the cars. The car-park attendant came out of his hut to see them off.

And then the rain came.

Patrick waited in the darkness until the car had gone and the man had returned to his hut. After a few minutes he walked up to the entrance coming in on the side of the building so that he was hidden from observation from the hut. There was no one in the entrance.

He stepped inside but he didn't go into the hall. He unbuttoned his coat and came striding out towards the parked cars, pulling his coat round as if he had just put it on.

He moved in the direction of the third row of cars and saw the car-park attendant heading across to him. Patrick stopped and took a two-shilling piece from his pocket. He moved back a pace, holding out his hand. The man understood.

"Don't bother to stay out and get soaked," Patrick said to him in easy tones. "I can see myself out. I'm close to the road."

"Very good sir," the man said, taking the coin, and saluting.

Patrick reached the Vauxhall and climbed inside fitting in the ignition-key.

He saw the attendant shut himself in his hut, and pulled the starter. He reversed out quickly and drove down to Eastern Avenue, turning eastward, deciding to fill the tank at Brentwood.

He had one bad moment at Maylands when he thought there was a police-car on his tail, but his anxious speculation about the vehicle in his mirror was removed when the car turned off at Brentwood.

But it had given him an anxious few minutes, and he drove on to Chelmsford before stopping for petrol.

He felt better after that. He began to congratulate himself when he got on to the quieter Braintree road. He drove confidently, deeper into the night.

Sixteen

Police-constable Webb's beat took in the parish of Hanniford as well as the territory covered by Hickham, which it adjoined. It meant a good many miles each time duty took him round his area, but he'd always enjoyed cycling.

Webb was content enough with his rural life. He was young and newly married, and while he appreciated that a country beat wouldn't offer the same number of cases and therefore, a lesser proportion of successful prosecutions which would be duly accorded in his favour when promotion was assessed, it had other compensations.

He and his wife had a new house and a nice bit of garden. The house was in the village, stood on its own, and was pretty modern, and that was worth something to a married couple with the price of property it was and labour-saving houses difficult to come by. True, most of his job was plain routine, issuing licences for the movement of livestock, signing movement order books, following up the village boys' raid on local orchards or waiting in the plantation to catch the youngsters red-handed as they cut the winter trees for firewood. Hardly the action and excitement, he imagined, of a busy town beat.

Webb had enjoyed his term at Divisional Headquarters, but when he married his one ambition was a posting to a rural section and a house of his own. So far as duties were concerned he wasn't looking forward to a life of thrills, he was quite satisfied to settle down to a hum-drum existence for a time, making the best of the opportunities that came his way.

It gave a man a chance to start a family. Despite the lack of sensational cases, he considered that his beat held a greater responsibility and demanded more initiative. The village policeman worked more on his own. Success in this task should bring promotion in due course.

That was how he saw it, and he could think of less important ambitions than working towards the job of section sergeant. And there was the occasional excitement of a country-house raid. Many wealthy people living in magnificent homes were a temptation to the criminal.

He knew two or three such fine places in his own district,

and there was always the likelihood of thwarting a big job, and because of his special local knowledge of playing an important part in it, perhaps getting himself and Hickham into the headlines of the national press, and just recognition by his superiors of his enthusism and abilities; and with this end in view, he took his duties zealously, he could see the promotion-ladder from the pattern in which the county force was administered. From police head-quarters down through the divisions under the control of superintendents, to the sub-divisions in the charge of inspectors which in turn were sub-divided into sections under the charge of section sergeants who controlled the beats.

P.C. Webb now had his foot on the first rung of the ladder. He was the village policeman. He thought it a good starting point. He had been at Hickham just over six months. Nothing sensational had fallen across his beat in that time.

Now, as he cycled along the quiet lanes in the early hours of the cold March morning towards the conference point where he met his section sergeant, he wondered if the sergeant would have anything further to report on the news flash that had come through before Webb had left his home.

A prisoner had escaped from escort while being taken from Peterborough to Norwich. All stations had been alerted, but it was in the East Anglian area that the man was most likely to be found. There had been a description. The man was not a habitual criminal. He had no record. He had merely panicked and got away.

More than likely the man would make for his home near Peterborough and would soon be rounded up. Webb wasn't expecting to find him in his district, but he was on the alert for any strange character or vehicle he encountered. So far he'd seen nothing to attract his attention.

The rain had stopped, though it had fallen steadily for nearly three hours after midnight. His wet cape still glistened in the light of his cycle lamp which reflected faintly from the road. The heavy clouds rolled away to the east and the stars appeared, glimmering like pale, distant lanterns in the velvet blackness of the sky.

With the passing of the clouds the wind quietened and became no more than a cold wave of air crisp and fresh with the aftermath of rain.

There were no lights to be seen, the hedgerows formed uneven and unbroken lines of deep shadow on either side. Somewhere across the fields a dog barked and went to sleep again. Now and again the dark outline of a roadside cottage slipped by as Webb glided silently past. In a farmyard cartshed an owl hooted mournfully and was answered from the trees sheltering the horse-pond. Nothing else stirred, not even the branches of the trees in the plantation he was passing.

Conference point was on the western limits of Webb's beat. It was a place of minor cross-roads. There was nothing there except the remains of a thatched barn; but it had been arranged as one of the suitable positions where police-constable and section sergeant met during their night duty.

So long as Webb made his conference points and met his sergeant at the appointed times and places, he was free to plan his routine and his method of patrolling his beat in his own manner. Unless there was some development and the sergeant had certain instructions for him, the meeting was short and each man then went on his own way.

P.C. Webb always liked to try and time his arrival a minute or two before his sergeant; it showed his keenness and awareness for punctuality. As he pulled up and dismounted at the signpost he saw the light of a cycle heading towards him from the other direction, and a few seconds later the burly figure of the sergeant dismounted beside him.

Sergeant Long had a full fleshy face with a bristling moustache. He had spent the best part of his fifty years in the Force. He was a bit old-fashioned, a stickler for discipline, but always fair and just. He was always ready to recognize the good qualities in his juniors.

P.C. Webb got along well with him, always precise and respectful in his presence. He stood before him smartly and reported all quiet, and listened attentively while Long told him that the escaped prisoner had been caught. He hadn't any details, but the news had come through before he left the station.

"Are the instructions for stopping cars cancelled then, Sergeant?"

The other shook his head. "Been some trouble at a road-house near Romford. Car stolen from the park during a dinner and dance. A place called the *Spinning Wheel* off Eastern Avenue."

He opened his notebook and switched on his torch. P.C. Webb's interest quickened. "Nothing to go on as yet," the sergeant said, consulting his notebook. "It was taken some time between eight o'clock last night and two-thirty this morning. A Vauxhall."

He began to reel off the few details and Webb took them down in his own book. He wrote in the owner's name, the registered number of the car and the colour.

"All stations are alerted," Sergeant Long told him. "So far there's no trace of the direction the thief took."

"Can't see what reason he'd have to head this direction," Webb said, closing his book. "But I'll keep my eyes open. Any other instructions, Sergeant?"

"No; I'll be in touch with you soon as I get further news."

A few minutes later P.C. Webb was continuing his lonely tour.

In a roundabout way he was heading for home. Although nothing had happened he'd had a wet, cold and tiring night; a typical night, and in the last hour his thoughts always strayed ahead of him, to the warm, cosy house, his waiting slippers and an appetising breakfast.

Round the bend in the road the headlights of an approaching car suddenly alerted him.

He got off his bicycle and leaned it against the hedge. Flashing on his torch he stepped out into the middle of the road and as the car entered the few hundred yards of straight ahead, he waved the torch from side to side. His pulse was racing a little.

The car pulled up with a faint squeal of tyres and Webb flashed his light over it as he walked round to the driving seat.

It wasn't a Vauxhall. It was an MG saloon, and he recognized it.

The cheerful grin of the young chap who lowered the window was recognizable, too, and so was his pretty companion in the passenger seat.

"Well, if it isn't P.C. Webb. Haven't you anything better to do than to stop people getting to bed?"

"Sorry to hold you up, sir." Webb was grinning in the darkness, he knew the couple well. They ran a small pig farm on the outskirts of Hickham. "Only doing my duty. Looking for a stolen car."

"Anybody we know?" The young man sounded more serious.

"Stolen near London. But we have to take action just in case."

"That's the worst of those engagement parties," the driver's wife said. "They just go on and on. We didn't leave Royston till three-thirty. And we've got to be up again at half-past-six."

"Just when you're going to bed," the driver of the MG smiled up at Webb.

"If I'm lucky, sir."

He watched the twin tail-lights of the MG fade out round the bend in the road, then he continued his journey.

A faint glimmer of light began to feather its way across the eastern sky, and cheerless though it was, P.C. Webb welcomed it. The stars began to fade and the landscape's dark shadows softened to the grey substance of trees and fence and the mellowed brick of cottage and farmhouse.

He still had a long ride ahead of him. His muscles were tired and his eyes smarted from the wind and the rain of the night. But the miles were always shorter in the morning light, and the strange shapes of the dark hours took on their old familiar appearance under the pale sky that heralded the new day.

Soon the chimney pots of the cottages would be smoking and the kettles on the stoves would be whistling for the tea. The thought took P.C. Webb's mind ahead to his own kitchen where in another hour his wife would be preparing for his arrival.

He pushed more strongly on his pedals. He could almost smell the bacon in the frying-pan.

Seventeen

Myra tried to relax against the luxurious upholstery of the back seat as the Rolls-Bentley ate up the straight miles of the A.45, but the further they drove from Hickham the more tense she became.

She had spent the weekend in reflection. Mrs. Hull had been more tiresome than usual, and her imaginative complaints had demanded more attention. Myra had duly fussed around her, sympathising and refuting the other woman's suggestions about the lines around her eyes, the encroaching wrinkles, the hint of a double-chin and everything else that occurred to her.

Mrs. Hull was a neurotic all right, a hypochondriac. She thought she had a fatty heart, and the headaches she often imagined she had she knew were due to blood-pressure. She was sure she suffered from most of the coronary diseases when all she needed, Myra knew, was a little exercise and a reduction in her chocolate intake. There was about her still a trace of the beauty she had once been, but she had let her muscles run to fat and had too much alcohol in her blood. It was all her hairdressers and beauticians could do to keep the grey hairs at bay, the sagging flesh under control.

Myra had seen the slow but sure march of deterioration even in the short time she had been her personal maid. She was not surprised that Jimmy Hull had sought his amorous adventures elsewhere. That Myra had herself become the object of his affections was one factor indicating it was time for her to be moving on.

And then Ted Patrick had come on the scene again.

She had never been able to forget him, never been able to eradicate the longing she always felt for him. The affair with Jimmy Hull was no more than a casual interlude. Half-reluctant she had let it take its course because that was easier than fighting; than losing the material benefits it brought. But she knew there could be no future in it.

Whereas with Ted there was a future. She believed he meant what he said now. To settle down and go straight.

She'd been happy to play along with Ted at the beginning. She'd been in the same racket, not the snatch, but the slower, less risky confidence-trick.

Falling for Ted had begun to change all that. She'd wanted to settle down, and she'd wanted him with her, not in jail. She'd started to get him round to her way of looking at things. But he had gone to Canada for a job, and she hadn't heard any more.

If she hadn't been able to forgive him for that, she couldn't forget him either, and she had thrown herself into an attempt to go straight in an effort to do so. The job in Nice had brought her into contact with the Hulls, and she had moved in with them. Jimmy Hull had been attentive from the start, and he had treated her well, partly to compensate for the niggling temperament of his wife to which she was subjected, and partly for his own ends.

It had been fun in the sun and gaiety of the Riviera, but it had already begun to die in the cold March winds of Suffolk. She knew the showdown had to come, and when it did, she'd want to get away.

Now she had her chance.

On Sunday, she had thought she ought to take the opportunity of doing a bit of rehearsing of her part in the job planned for Tuesday morning. Hull was out, over at Burnham, to see how his new yacht was shaping in the builder's yard; his wife had gone over to Thetford to spend the afternoon with friends; and the servants weren't around. She went into the library and tried the lock and bolts on the french window. She noted with satisfaction that they had a free, smooth movement and made no noise. She opened the window a few inches. It moved without a creak. She decided it was wiser not to go outside and time herself over the short distance from the terrace to the spot where she had told Ted to leave the car. Someone might see her and wonder what she was doing using the library french windows when there were other ways into the garden. And anyway, all outside work was Ted's pigeon.

She closed the window and went into the hall. It was light and spacious. The inside of the wide front door was painted cream and matched the light distempered walls and the white banisters and stairs. The polished surface of the dark oak boarded floor was almost obscured by white rugs and a biscuit-coloured carpet.

Plenty of room to move, Ted should be inside and up the stairs in a matter of seconds. Even though the lay-out of the place was unfamiliar to him.

Myra took her time, pausing on the landing for a moment before opening Mrs. Hull's bedroom door. She went in, closed the door and crossed to the dressing-table.

She took up the diamond and sapphire ring and examined it, wondering what its value was. It wasn't one of her best rings. The diamonds were too small and too few; but even disposing of it in the way in which Ted had to, it should fetch a hundred or two. She returned the ring and lifted the lid of the jewellery-case.

Myra knew what she would find. She had tidied up when Mrs. Hull had finished dressing and had helped to put on the diamond clip, ear-rings and the rope of pearls. In the case were what Mrs. Hull would call odds and ends. Two pendants, a clip, two rings and an emerald and pearl necklace. It wasn't the best stuff.

She crossed and glanced into the dressing-room. It was a small room in the same pale pink as the bedroom. It had one window. There was a small mahogany writing table alongside it. A long, frameless wall mirror reflected the wardrobe and the other pieces consisted of an arm-chair, a pair of Hepplewhite chairs, and a tallboy. The carpet covered the whole floor.

Myra closed the dressing-room door again and moved slowly to the bed. Above the reading lamp was a small oval, gilt-framed picture of an Edwardian actress, a so-called great-aunt of Mrs. Hull. Behind the picture was the wall safe.

She could visualize what lay in it. In her imagination she saw this other jewel-case, the clasp and the lid sprang up, revealing an assortment of stones in which the glitter of diamonds predominated, all in various settings. Emeralds, pearls, rubies and sapphires, all to open the gates of her future with Ted.

She had turned away from the bedside, her gaze straying through the windows and out over the front lawns to the open drive gates. She began to imagine Ted's arrival on Tuesday morning, she could see herself opening the library-window. She imagined the consternation and inquiries when the raid had been discovered. She would be questioned. Had she heard anything in the night? In the early hours?

Her heart had suddenly contracted. Supposing the police suggested it was an inside job? How would she be able to prove that she was in bed? Although there was nothing to connect her with Ted, she might be a suspect if she was in the house at the time. Better to be out of the way. She'd feel safer.

She could leave everything set, just as they had planned. If the french window was unlocked, Ted could let himself in. He didn't need her around while he handled the job. He knew the layout, where the sparklers were kept.

But how could she be out? What reason could she give Ted? Where could she go?

She had stood gazing out at the chestnut trees, and then suddenly the way to fix it had suggested itself.

She could go to Newmarket with Jimmy Hull. Since they had been back from the South of France and he'd begun visiting his trainer, he had promised to take her with him on some occasion. He had burbled on at her about the early mornings on Newmarket Heath, and the hundreds of horses at their exercise. It was a sight to thrill the heart of any sportsman. That's what he'd said.

She had said she'd like to go with him, without much show of enthusiasm. But she could remind him of it.

She could think of no reason why he should refuse to take her Tuesday morning. Mrs. Hull would be in bed until her usual time and if they weren't back until around midday it would be okay.

He would be thrilled to find her willing to get up so early just to watch the horses; he would think it was because she wanted to be with him.

She could cope with that.

She would take the first opportunity to ask him, and lay it on. That night or in the morning. Afterwards she would ring Ted; sometime to-morrow, before three. She didn't intend to tell him the real reason why she wouldn't be there to let him in. She'd make some excuse.

It wouldn't worry him, so long as she left everything okay for him.

In the close proximity of the Rolls-Bentley she had been

prepared to be on her guard; to be watchful that her eyes and face gave Jimmy Hull no clue to what was going on behind the mask of her face. Her fears and hopes, her feverish speculations. It was easier than she'd expected.

Jimmy Hull was asleep.

Myra had awakened before day-break, dressed and hurried down to the kitchen to prepare tea and biscuits for Hull and the chauffeur. As the sky lightened she had returned to her room to open the curtains and signal the all clear for Ted Patrick when he came, and then came her stealthy visit to the library to unbolt and unlock the french window.

Hull had been out on a bit of a party the night before and had returned late. When she took up his tea and spent some time smoothing the sleep out of him, he had awakened with a headache which had put him in a sullen mood.

The chauffeur had been waiting in the drive, the engine ticking over silently, for Myra and Hull to appear. Myra had hung back until Hull had gone out, and then making a final check to reassure herself that all was ready, she had followed. The Rolls-Bentley had swung out of the gates with Hull already dozing in his corner, and headed towards the Newmarket road.

Hull continued to sleep heavily as the car ghosted along. He breathed noisily through his nose, drowning the whispering sound of the airflow around the car. He was a powerfully built man in his early forties, and had managed to retain his good looks and dark hair, but his figure had run to seed a bit.

He was recognized as a great sporting personality, a good golfer and rider. His sailing was done in only the best climates, he had always been able to afford to do things the easy way. His money smoothed the path. His thickening figure proved how successful he was.

Myra knew that behind the gloss and the charm, he was really low; but she felt no bitterness towards him. She had gone into it with her eyes open, knowing it would come to nothing and get her nowhere.

She had no thought of revenge in joining up with Ted Patrick. It was just the one and only way of finding permanent happiness, of mending the wild, broken threads of her life, and Ted's. Jimmy Hull's wife's loot was the means to that end. She had no compunction about taking it. Only a nervous tension now the moment had come. Something she could remember from the old days at the game. The consolation that it was the last time helped her through the ordeal.

She was glad that Jimmy Hull was snoring, instead of pawing her over.

She sat in the corner of the seat, her elbow on the rest, chin cupped in her hand, staring out at the passing country. It hadn't been easy to ask Hull to take her along, she hadn't any reasonable excuse, apart from reminding him of his offer. She'd picked a lucky moment the previous afternoon when he had had a phone message from his trainer that the new colt had arrived.

She had come into the hall just as he had finished talking to the trainer and confirming the morning visit. She had asked him then. He had told her that, of course, she would be welcome if she didn't mind the early start.

It had been as easy as that. And from that moment on she had gone about her preparations with a new confidence.

Hull had been out for the rest of the day, returning in the early hours. Mrs. Hull had retired early and had knocked back her sleeping-draught with as much relish as if it were a glass of gin.

Myra had waited until she'd heard the other's stertorous breathing then she had checked the whereabouts of the jewellery-case. Sometimes Mrs. Hull would take the whole lot of stuff out of the wall-safe and gloat over it, and fall asleep without putting it back. But the jewellery-case was nowhere around when Myra went into Mrs. Hull's bedroom, and she felt pretty sure it must be in the safe. Satisfied, she had gone to bed herself, and despite the restless night she had awakened fresh long before it was time to get up.

Everything had gone smoothly from the outset, and there was no reason now for the hot feeling of tension that tightened her insides. She knew it was her imagination at work, visualizing Ted's arrival at the house, wondering if he would leave behind some clue fastening suspicion on them both.

The gently undulating wooded terrain racing past revealed its lonely beauty in the strengthening light of the early morning. It had no quietening influence on her pent-up emotion of fears and doubts. She stared out of the window, wishing the journey over.

Hull came to as they turned at the clock tower in New-market and drove up a twisting road that led up on to the Heath. The car stopped at the wrought-iron gates of a compact red-brick house, the last building in the road, and over-looking the green heathland which swept up to the horizon in a gentle rise, topped by islands of trees, and worn with the tracks of countless horses. But at that early hour, except for a stray dog wandering in the direction of the main road, the area was deserted.

"We'll find Jackson in his office," Hull said, as Myra followed him out of the car. They left the chauffeur settling down for a quiet smoke, and walked back along the road a few yards to where the high brick wall ended in wide double-gates.

Hull led the way into a small macadam surface yard in which was parked two horse boxes, but there was little else here to suggest a trainer's premises. A further wall flanked it in which were another pair of gates leading into the paddock and the stabling block. On the right, just inside from the street, was a small office building of old brick, its door, window frames and timbered gables painted a dark green. As they approached, the door opened and a broad-shouldered slim-waisted man appeared, dressed in breeches, riding boots, a tweed hacking-jacket and grey sweater.

Jackson was past middle-age, but he had the stature and looks of a man ten years younger. His face was bronzed by wind and sun, and in contrast under the shaggy brows and wide-peaked cap his eyes were the lightest blue. He carried an ivory-handled riding crop and he tapped this gently against the side of his breeches as he came out to greet them.

Hull introduced Myra and explained how she wanted to see how race horses trained.

"The stable-boys have just started," Jackson said, his eyes scanning Myra appreciatively. "So you'll see what goes on before exercise." He turned to Hull, smiling. "But about the new colt. He's in good shape. Just a little nervous after his journey yesterday."

He opened one of the inner gates, and stood to one side as Hull and Myra stepped on to a straw-covered concrete track running alongside the long single-storey block of stables. The two men went ahead talking and Myra followed a pace or two behind, her thoughts temporarily away from Hickham.

The stabling took up two sides of a large paddock which was enclosed on the other two sides by the garden wall of the house and the wall separating it from the open heath. The short grass of the paddock looked young and fresh, sparkling with moisture as the light frost melted in the rising temperature. The sun had begun its climb above the eastern horizon.

There were thirty stables overlooking the paddock. The stable-lads in breeches and jerseys, moved to and fro as they carried bundles of straw or sieves of oats and bran and hay from the small two-storey granary sandwiched between the stables in the main block, to their charges, each lad having two horses under his care.

There were three young girls on the stable staff and they worked with as much zest and efficiency as the boys.

The routine at Jackson's was typical of the trainer's day. With such valuable, sensitive animals under his charge it was no wonder the drill was strict and work went with a clock-like precision.

At six a.m. the stable-boys arrived and went to work under the control of the head boy. The stables were cleaned out, the horses attended to and fed, and the first morning's exercise on the heath followed for about an hour and a half. They returned to the stables where the horses were cleaned and groomed, the staff then having breakfast before preparing the second string of horses which took their exercise during the mid-morning.

Out on the heath the routine was walking, trotting, cantering and sometimes galloping, depending on what the trainer considered each horse required. Some of the boys and girls were not considered suitable riders or as yet strong enough to control a thoroughbred in a gallop and when horses were selected for this exercise, their riders had to be changed.

The horses were always ridden with the same weights, the jockeys weighing eight-stone seven pounds or eight-stone nine pounds. In some cases when a fresh horse had joined the string and it was necessary to find what the animal was capable of there would be a run-off with another horse which had already proved itself.

And it was this that Jackson suggested to Hull as they

stood at the open stable door, gazing on the colt that had arrived the day before.

Myra thought that *Even Chance* was a handsome-looking creature, with a smooth dark coat. Its lithe body and long slender legs revealed grace and power. It lifted its head from the manger and turned to look at them as they stood just inside his stable, its ears flicking forward, sensing that strangers were present. It had a dark well-proportioned head with a white patch just above the eyes.

The stable-boy finished brushing and straightened the rug over the horse's back.

"How is he?"

"All right now, sir. He's quietened down a lot. Seems to have had a good night."

Jackson gave the boy a nod, as Hull and Myra went forward and stroked the horse's muzzle. He flicked his head away from them as if in mild protest, until the boy cooed some words into his ear and patted his shoulder. Then he stood while his owner and Myra gently coaxed him.

"All right," Jackson said. "Get him ready."

They moved along the block and Jackson examined another horse which had been off its feed. He checked the animal's temperature with the stable-boy and satisfaction showed in his face when he found it was now normal.

"Running a bit of a temperature yesterday evening," Jackson said to Hull. "He left most of his afternoon feed and I was getting a bit worried about him. But he's making out all right now. Very temperamental, these thorough-breds."

"I know," Hull said with a sly grin at Myra. "Sensitive and particular, like women."

Myra smirked at him, her thoughts miles away. How was the caper going at the house?

They continued along the block, looking into two or three more of the stables where the boys were saddling up, and then stood near the exit gates on to the heath, talking. A boy opened the gates and another lad brought along the hack that Jackson was to ride and stood in the background waiting while the horses slowly trooped out.

Jackson suggested that Myra and Hull should move up to a high point on the heath where they would be in a good position to see the exercise. It would also give them an appetite for breakfast, to which he invited them to join him at the house afterwards.

The heath was now alive with horses and their riders. Long strings of them in Indian file moved at different speeds, walking, trotting, cantering. As one group of riders slowly vanished over Warren Hill, or disappeared behind a straggling copse, another line filed into view, heading back down the track towards the town.

Hull was familiar with the layout. He'd been on the heath before.

Myra fell into step beside him as he set a brisk walking pace along the macadam road winding through the turf and up into the trees topping the hill. At a point just over half way they stopped and looked across at a stretch called the Gallops. They could see Jackson walking his team gently along the lower edge of the heath.

"If he's going to run off, it'll be over there." Hull indicated the Gallops. "I'm going over for a closer look." He glanced down at Myra's shoes and then at the turf which was soft, and well-trodden in places, after the night's rain. "Are you coming?"

"Not in these shoes, Jimmy," she said, "if you don't mind. I'll watch from here."

He grinned and marched away, his heavy brogues sinking into the soggy patches.

A string of some twenty horses passed slowly in front of her cutting Hull's figure from view. The graceful, rhythmic movements as the creatures walked sedately past were a sharp contrast to the youthful grins and idle chatter of their riders.

The heath was bright with the steady, glorious beat of freedom. The air was fresh and crisp and seemed to cleanse the insides with every breath the lungs sucked down. It gave Myra a heady intoxicating feeling that drowned every grim reality. She felt the strengthening warmth of the sun as it climbed above the trees, throwing a strange pattern of shadows over bracken and fern as its rays struck the naked branches.

Myra turned her gaze on the town.

She could see Jackson's house and the neighbouring premises of other trainers fringing the lower end of the heath, and beyond was a kaleidoscopic pattern of the Newmarket's roofs.

And almost everywhere in between moved even lines of horses.

After the first few minutes the novelty and beauty of the scene began to fade, Myra realized that she was no longer watching. She was conscious of the wave of doubts seeping into her mind, driving out the exhilarating feeling and leaving only the hangover of fear.

There was the tension tightening again inside her that she had temporarily lost. Her legs felt weak and her eyes were drawn towards the east.

She knew she couldn't stand still much longer. Her thoughts of Ted, the mental picture of the house at Hickham assailed her with renewed, insistent force. A score of questions curled up in her mind and dissolved without solution. She wanted to turn and dash back to the house. See if the job was done. But there'd be no way of knowing until the morning had gone. She had to content herself with the knowledge that he wouldn't let her down. But standing there alone on the heath made her restless and riddled with anxiety. She must do something.

She pulled her coat tighter about her and stepped on to the road.

She began to walk purposefully down the hill to Jackson's place.

Eighteen

Always turn the dial slowly and evenly; never whirl it round or jerk it. If he turned past a combination number, or was uncertain of the number of turns he had made, or jerked the dial backwards in course of turning, he would have to recommence the whole procedure from the beginning. This applied, he knew, both to normal opening and to setting a new combination.

It would be like taking candy from a baby. While the baby was asleep. He grinned to himself in the semi-darkness. The only sound in the house was the stertorous breathing of the sleeper in the bed, above which was the wall-safe. The heavy snoring filled the bedroom.

Ted Patrick flexed his fingers in their black silk gloves.

The night journey had been uneventful. His arrival timed to a nicety. Myra's signal had been at the green and the french window had been awaiting his silent touch on the handle. He'd found the bedroom without a hitch.

It was a case of walking through a house that he'd already been through many times in his mind. Every few paces he'd paused, listening, but he had heard nothing. Now he stood motionless in the bedroom staring at the oval, gilt-framed picture, with the old girl sleeping off the dose Myra had administered. He felt confident as he stood there, grinning to himself in the darkness, the fortune that was about to drop into his hands.

Thanks to Myra's sound planning; yes, he had to hand it to her. He was glad she was out of the way. He'd only got himself to think about now. Only himself to consider if anything should go wrong while he was on the job. But what could go wrong? The whole set-up was foolproof.

He moved in close and lifted off the picture of the Edwardian actress.

It was a Chubb Size Five wall peter all right, designed to protect treasures from the average housebreaker. Secured by specially stout bolts, it was built into the wall so that it was an integral part of the structure of the house, and all the rest of it. But it didn't matter a damn to him that the doorplate was made of solid steel, with additional drill-resisting reinforcement over the entire area of the lock-case, and the lock itself was further protected by steel plate, the door fitted with three moving bolts three quarters of an inch in diameter, controlled by a 3-wheel type keyless combination lock. The safe was enamelled grey, and it was recessed so that the dial did not jut out beyond the wall and push into the back of the picture. The circle of light from his pencil-torch showed the star marking the outer ring of the dial and the setting mark at the side of the star for use when changing the combination; and it didn't matter a damn to him, because he had the combination numbers pat in his head.

Could the woman really have left the combination set on three numbers as it had been dispatched from the factory? Ten, twenty, thirty? It didn't seem possible that she could have been so foolish. Especially as he knew Chubb's must have warned her to change it to her own combination. But people did that, despite all advice and warnings. They were so afraid of not being able to remember the new numbers and being unable to unlock the safe. That was why they did the next stupid thing by writing down the numbers and keeping the slip of paper where it could be found by anyone nosy.

He would know any minute now if Mrs. Hull had been doubly stupid. Keeping the factory combination, and jotting the numbers down in her diary, for fear she would forget them, and had to get in touch with Chubb's and admit she hadn't taken their urgent advice and changed the number. No fool like a fool who didn't want to be thought a fool.

Ted Patrick's black silk-gloved fingers closed round the dial.

He turned the dial anti-clockwise, stopping when the first number came the fourth time to the star. He turned the dial clockwise, stopping when the second number came the third time to the star. He turned the dial anti-clockwise, stopping when the third number came the second time to the star. He turned the dial clockwise slowly until it stopped. The lock was unlocked.

Patrick's grin became a smirk of triumph as he slipped the last article from the jewellery case into his pocket It was a diamond encrusted bracelet which glittered with fire as he turned it in the light from his torch. He pushed the jewel-case back into the safe and silently closed the door.

He hung the gilt, oval picture over the recess and turned to glance at Mrs. Hull. He could make out her open mouth in the pale blob that was her face.

There was a time to stay and there was a time to go and this was a time to go. Already the grey light of dawn was shot with the rays of the rising sun, whose fingers were beginning to creep round the edges of the curtains. It was no time to linger to congratulate himself. He had a long way to go, and the sooner he started on the road back before life was astir, the better his chances to ditch the car unseen.

Outside on the landing he paused in the shadows which were melting as the light strengthened and filtered through the landing windows and up from the hall. But now that he was separated from the sound of Mrs. Hull's noisy slumber, silence reigned.

There was only the faint swish-swish of his belted raincoat as he went quickly down the stairs, along to the back of the hall into the library and out on to the terrace. He glanced quickly towards the garage. The doors were flung wide and the place deserted as when he had stolen on to the terrace ten minutes before. From one of the open windows of the outbuildings came the plaintive mewing of a cat; but there was nothing else. The sky was brightening with a scarlet glow.

He moved round the corner of the house and along the side wall. No one passed in the road. Half-a-dozen paces took him into the shrubbery. He moved silently through it and reached the car. He got in and closed the door quietly. He started the engine and drove slowly on to the drive and down it to the road.

Patrick drove through the silent village, taking the road back to the A.45 along which Myra had directed him on Friday afternon. It was the shortest route to the fast Newmarket road, and speed now was essential. He had less than an hour to make the chalk quarry outside Ipswich. Once he was on the main road he could let the Vauxhall rip.

But his objective was nearly three miles away, at the end of the narrow twisting lane. He had to keep his speed down. He half-expected around any bend to meet a farm-worker on his way to work, or a farm cart or even a milk lorry. He couldn't afford a hold-up in an accident. That would finish him.

But he didn't meet anything or anybody, until he came

within a few hundred yards of the major road. Then the uniformed figure dismounting from a bicycle and stepping out into the road signalling him to stop sent shivers of panic shooting through his stomach and down into his toes.

Automatically his foot eased off the accelerator; but he knew he dare not stop. The realization of some trap thundered in his head. The loss of the car had been discovered, he told himself. Maybe the police had some clue that it was in the Suffolk area. Every copper had been alerted.

Or maybe, they'd had only a warning. Maybe they didn't know where it was, and this was just one bright copper who stopped any stranger on his beat so early in the morning. The thoughts flashed through his mind in the space of seconds. Whichever way it was he couldn't risk it. And the faster he drove the less chance the copper would have to get his number. He'd be too busy jumping out of the way.

Patrick pushed hard down on the throttle and the car leaped forward.

The copper wasn't quick enough. His attempt to jump aside was thwarted by his bicycle which he was still holding. Patrick turned at the last minute in an attempt to avoid the uniformed figure, but he'd left it too late. There was a thud and then a clatter as the front bumper and off-side wing hit the man and the machine.

Patrick had a momentary glimpse of a buckled bicycle wheel, a flying police helmet and helpless, waving arms, Then it was all over and he was past.

He saw in the mirror the twisted shape lying close to the grass verge, his broken cycle around him.

He brought the car to a stop. His hands were shaking on the steering wheel and sweat made blobs on his forehead and began running down his face. He had to go back and see if the man was dead. And he couldn't leave him in the road. Someone would find him. Maybe within minutes.

He reversed a few yards. Stopped and got out, running back reluctantly to the scene. A glance told him the copper was dead. Blood streamed from an ugly wound above the temple. One arm lay twisted under him. The face was ashen in the changing light, and one eye was open staring sightlessly up at the sky.

Nineteen

He was the local copper. And once he was found there would be a hue-and-cry extended far beyond his village. Patrick jolted himself into action. He felt over the man's heart Not a flicker. He pulled the body over the grass verge, across the ditch and through the hedge. He looked round, finding himself at the edge of a small plantation. Between the hedge and the trees the ground was dotted with dwarf bushes and fern.

He dragged the body nearer the trees and lay it behind one of the bushes. Then he went back for the wreckage of the bicycle and the helmet. He left them close to the body, and tried to cover up the break he'd made in the hedge. But there was no time for perfection. And there was nothing he could do about the bloodstains at the side of the road or the broken glass of the cycle-lamps.

He ran back to the car, opened the door, then realized there might be bloodstains on the bumper. He moved round to the front. There was no trace of blood, but the off-side half of the bumper was twisted and the front wing dented. The force of the impact had pushed the headlamp back slightly and the glass was badly cracked. But it wasn't too noticeable. No one was going to have an opportunity for a good look at it. And there were plenty of cars on the road with dents.

He drove away quickly and on to the major road. He met nothing on the short, fast drive to Bury St Edmunds. He began looking out for the turning past the barracks which would take him outside the town centre.

As he approached it he saw a uniformed figure cycling just ahead of him, and he cursed to himself when he saw the cop turn on to the road he was planning to take. He daren't get near him. It was risky just to overtake him. There was nothing for it but to risk driving through the town centre.

The traffic lights were red. The thought of a wait gave him the jitters again. He pulled up close to the tailboard of a lorry. There were one or two people about now. But they took no notice of him. And he didn't see another cop.

When the lights changed he crept forward with the lorry. He kept close to it across the next pair of lights and along the narrow street. He got some comfort from the knowledge that the lorry was a useful screen. His frequent glances in the mirror showed him that nothing was behind.

He was glad the lorry was going his way. He remained close on its tail through the remainder of the town. He had to keep his eye on the signboards until he recognized the now deserted Angel Hill and the old Abbey gateway.

He kept behind the lorry until they had cleared the round-about and were heading down the Ipswich road. Then he pulled out and shot ahead.

There were a few vehicles on the road but his driving mirror remained comfortably clear. Nothing came up on his tail to give him anxious thoughts of police-cars. He would have felt better if he could have avoided the next two small towns that lay across his route to the quarry, and although he considered the roads leading off the main road, he daren't risk taking one. He would avoid the towns only to lose himself in the heart of the country, which was peppered with lanes and by-roads in which any hurrying stranger would find himself going in circles in his attempt to reach his destination.

Patrick hadn't got the time for such diversions. He'd got to stick to his route and take his chance.

The unforeseen accident with the local copper hadn't changed his plans; only made more imperative their execution. Once the car was safely dumped there'd be no need for panic. The police in the London area would be particularly alert for the stolen car, but he couldn't see that the Suffolk police would be taking any special precautions. Not until the body had been found.

He was banking on it going undetected for another hour. Nevertheless, as he approached Stowmarket he began to get the jitters again, and it was all he could do to keep his nerves in check.

But there were no hold-ups. Even the traffic-lights were green when he got to them, and he drove through the almost empty main street at the regulation speed limit. Once out of the town he kept the needle in the sixty region, and less than ten minutes later was passing along the wide thoroughfare of Needham Market.

Everything continued smoothly until he reached the turning leading up to the chalk quarry, then came a minor but irritating delay. The turning for which he watched anxiously was suddenly pin-pointed by two cyclists ahead who turned off the major road on to it. He went by slowly, watching the backs of the two men as they peddalled up the rise. He cursed them silently. The time was six-thirty-five and he had got to wait until they had got beyond the quarry before he could venture near it.

He drove slowly on about a quarter-of-a-mile, stopped and lit a cigarette. It was his first smoke since he'd left the house, and he dragged at it deeply, as he turned round and drove slowly back, glancing impatiently at his watch.

More minutes ticked by, and then he was turning up the lane. He drove cautiously searching for any sign of the cyclists. He topped the rise and began a slow run down towards the edge of the quarry. He stopped the car at the old field gateway which he had previously marked, and cut the engine.

Nothing disturbed the stillness. The early morning hush was intensified by the crunch of his footsteps on the road as he got out of the car.

The air was crisp, but there was no wind. The two men had vanished somewhere ahead. A glance across the fields beyond the opposite hedge, showed them to be deserted; the quarry, too, was deserted and bathed in shadow. He went to the lip of the drop. The sudden cry of a bird startled him as it flew off its nest nearby, and skimmed above the mirror-like surface of the dark sinister-looking water.

Patrick considered the distance from the gateway to the quarry edge and noted the bumps in the gound. It was going to be quite an easy operation. He'd start the car off in low gear and hop out. It would take itself nicely over.

He hurried back to the road, started the engine and manoeuvred round into the gateway. He lined the car up, taking it within a few feet of the edge. Then dropping the lever into first gear he let the clutch in slowly, throwing the door open wide. As it crept forward he stepped out.

He stood motionless, fascinated by the spectacle, as the front wheels jerked off the edge into space, then tipped sharply downward and with a rending of metal the whole car lurched over and dived into the water with a thunderous splash that sent a cloud of rooks cawing into the air from the nearby elm trees. Slowly the car settled, its boot sinking down beneath the surface.

He watched until the wash had subsided, waiting for the after end of the roof to disappear, but it remained obstinately a few inches above the surface. He realized it would go no further; that he should have made some examination of the irregular depth of the bottom of the pit. But it was too late now. It was hidden from the road and the new workings of the quarry. And it might settle later. There was nothing else he could do but hope that no one ventured so far; and to get to hell out of it.

He stubbed out his cigarette on the heel of his shoe and then he ground it carefully into the soft earth. He lit a fresh one.

He made his way to the lane and walked briskly in the direction he had just come.

He glanced at his watch. The time was six-fifty.

Twenty

Ted Patrick reached Ipswich station with three minutes to spare. He had walked to the fringe of the town and caught a trolley-bus as far as the centre where he'd changed to another for the railway-station.

He joined the short queue at the booking-office and bought a single ticket to London. Then over to the bookstall for a couple of papers and through the barrier to mingle with the other passengers on the platform as the train steamed in.

The passengers were mostly men, though he did notice two or three women further along the platform. There were uniformed railway-workers going to an intermediate station. Business men with brief cases and rolled umbrellas in dark Homburg hats and well-cut overcoats. There was a soldier with a load of kit and a couple of R.A.F. types each carrying nothing more than a light canvas grip. There was an American serviceman with a flashy young woman, presumably heading for a day in London together.

Patrick felt more at ease among this motley collection, and he found himself relaxing a little. He was less conspicuous than walking the deserted country roads. And there was nothing in his appearance to make him look out of place. He was an ordinary type. Even his shoes didn't look as if they'd been out all night after he'd rubbed them over with a handkerchief. He was just one of a crowd, on his way to work.

There was going to be plenty of room on the train. As the train stopped with a grinding of brakes he was opposite the restaurant-car. He remembered then that he'd eaten nothing since he'd left the flat the previous afternoon. He got straight into the restaurant-car and sat in a window-seat at one of the tables. He pushed his hat on the rack but he didn't take his coat off. The precious weight of the loot in his pocket was nice to feel against his thigh. As he settled himself comfortably the train pulled out, and a white-coated man was at his side for his order.

When he had gone Patrick opened the morning papers, but he couldn't concentrate on the news. Now he began trying to justify the action he had taken that morning on the lonely Hickham road. Now that he was inactive and no urgent next step to claim all his attention, he couldn't keep the mental picture of that sprawled shape on the road from filling his mind.

He couldn't help what had happened. He hadn't intended running the copper down; but there had been no other course open to him than to drive straight on when he saw that the fool meant business. It was his own fault. He asked for it. Not moving till the last minute.

Patrick didn't go for violence, especially against the police. When a copper was killed they never rested till they'd pinched whoever had done the job. And if he was caught he'd never get away with it because everything would be against him. The stolen car, the robbery and the removal of the body in an attempt to cover the crime. One thing played off against another. He would have had his chips, if he was caught.

But they'd got to catch him and then pin it on him. And he'd covered his tracks well. Even when they found the car, there'd be nothing to link it with him or the death of the copper. He knew the police and was known to them; but before they could do a tiling they'd got to break his alibi.

Breakfast took his mind off things for a bit He'd ordered bacon-and-eggs with fried bread and sausages, followed by toast and marmalade washed down with coffee. He ate his way leisurely through it as the train sped towards London.

The girl sitting opposite who'd just come along for a coffee set him thinking again. She was a pretty blonde. She didn't notice Patrick. All she was conscious of was the cup of coffee before her and the paper-back novel in her hand. Patrick decided it must have been a fascinating story to claim such wrapt attention, but it gave him a chance to study her without being observed. She reminded him of Myra.

He lit a cigarette and tried to picture Myra at the trainer's place at Newmarket. Whatever she was doing there for Hull he felt sure she hadn't got her mind on it, she'd be wondering about him, her Ted. Worried stiff lest something should go wrong.

Nothing had gone wrong over the way he'd handled the peter. It was later he'd hit the trouble. How would Myra take it when she heard? When the police started questioning her?

There was no known link between the two of them, he reassured himself. No one knew they knew each other. And how could she know anything about the robbery or the accident when she was over at Newmarket? Hull would confirm everything she said. He was more pleased than ever now Myra hadn't been at the house that morning. He was confident he could count on her. She'd size the whole thing up and keep her mouth shut. And wait until she heard from him. If anything went wrong his end she'd keep out of it; lie low. If anything went wrong his end.

What could go wrong? Everything was covered. Nevertheless, he began to sweat a bit at the thought of the possibilities, and he was glad to get up as the train pulled in to Liverpool Street, and get out. Walking with the crowd down to the Metropolitan line took his mind off the subject.

He got an Inner Circle train, standing with a group of city-workers just inside the doors. The journey to Paddington was like an endless crawl of stopping and starting, but he passed the time working out his method of returning to the flat. He'd call at the local grocers, pick up a loaf of bread and one or two other things. To suggest that he'd just nipped out; and when he reached the mews anyone seeing him would conclude he had come out shopping.

He'd keep Price with him for lunch so that he could be in the picture about exactly what he had done and where he had been and the times, and Price could wander back to his own place in the afternoon as if having just made a friendly call.

When he came out of Paddington Station a cold drizzle had begun to soak the streets. He was thankful for it. It fitted in with his depressed mood and it made his appearance in a coat and hat natural even for a brief shopping expedition. He headed for Sussex Gardens, walking some distance along the wide thoroughfare before turning off and cutting through in the direction of the Bayswater Road. It meant a slight detour to reach the grocer's shop but he wanted to give the impression that he'd just come up from the flat.

He met no one he knew on the way. The unpleasant morning was keeping people indoors who didn't have to show themselves. The grocer's shop was empty but for one woman customer. Patrick bought a loaf and a packet of tea, exchanging a few words with the man behind the counter, planting that he wouldn't have been shopping on such a morning if he hadn't been low on tea. Having left the right impression behind him, Patrick made for the flat as quickly as possible.

There was no one else in the mews, though someone might have seen him from one of the windows. He let himself in and hurried upstairs. The living-room was empty, the curtains dividing it from the bedroom were pulled close.

Patrick dropped the stuff he was carrying on the table and called Price's name.

Twenty-One

There was no answer.

Ted Patrick stared round his eyes narrowed. Where the devil was Price? He couldn't have walked out on the job, panicked, that was too much to believe. A moment of apprehension flooded through him.

An incoherent grunt came from behind the curtains, and Patrick stepped across and pulled them aside.

Price was sprawled on the bed still wearing Patrick's clothes. His collar was unbuttoned and his tie loose. His hair was an untidy mass and every time he breathed bubbles foamed on his mouth. The jacket and trousers were crumpled and showed drink stains, but when Patrick glanced at the shoes they were still unmarked. The polish looked new as it had done the day previous, yet it had been raining.

With rough urgency Patrick leaned over and grabbed Price's shoulders.

"Harry," he said. "Harry, wake up."

Price snorted and twisted from the grip without opening his eyes, falling back on the bed.

Patrick shook him again more violently.

The other squirmed and opened one eye, which focused on him blankly. "Go 'way," he said thickly. "Can't you—let a feller sleep?" He sank back and was instantly asleep again.

His breath reeked of alcohol. As the truth began to dawn on him, Patrick turned back to the living-room.

He saw the empty bottle under the chair, where it had fallen. It was the one he'd poured the drinks from the day before. It had been three-quarters full. There was a soiled glass lying on its side on the carpet. On the sideboard was another used glass. Patrick sniffed it. There was the smell of gin. He opened the cupboard and lifted out the gin bottle. There was about enough in the bottle for a couple of small drinks.

Patrick could hardly believe the picture that rose up in his mind of Price lolling back in the arm-chair, soaking himself in the whisky and gin the whole night through. The very thing he had planned as the one great certainty, his alibi, now more important than ever, was non-existent. There must be some explanation, he tried to tell himself. The cards couldn't be stacked against him like this.

Price must have gone out and carried out the job according to plan, and then when he'd returned already half-shot he must have had a thirst for more. That was the answer. He'd got back in the early hours, seen the bottle and decided to have just one more. And it had led to another and another. Until he'd finished the bottle and started on the gin, finally drinking himself insensible.

But there were the shoes.

Fear and bitter fury filling him, Patrick went into the kitchen and got a bowl of cold water. There was no time to lose. He had to get Price on his feet and his mind awake. He had to know what had been going on.

He came back and stood over Price with the bowl slopping over. The man's reeking breath seemed to fill the little room.

"Price," Patrick said savagely.

There was a faint grunt but the figure on the bed hardly stirred.

"This'll make you talk," and Patrick sloshed the water full into the face that was turned up to him, mouth half-open, and the reaction was instantaneous.

Price lurched up gasping and spluttering wearing a wild, frightened look.

"What—what the—hell——?" He sat up shaking his head. He rubbed the water from his eyes, and passed his hand across his forehead. He looked shocked and scared. But he was awake and sober.

"You got some explaining to do. You drank yourself insensible on my whisky and gin. You'd better make with the talk."

Price covered his head with his hands. He couldn't look at Patrick.

"God—my head," he groaned.

"I want to know what happened," Patrick snarled impatiently. "When did you begin soaking yourself here? When you came back? Have you been out?"

"I can't—can't remember—"

Patrick clouted him once, twice round his jaw. Price drew back with a cry of pain.

"Better get your memory working," Patrick said. "Or I'll beat the living daylights out of you."

Price didn't know where to look. There was a shamed guilty expression on his face. He tried to cover it up by drying himself with a handkerchief. His eyes met Patrick's at last, but he couldn't meet the look for long. His gaze dropped to his hands as he rolled the handkerchief in nervous jerks.

"I—I followed the drill okay," he said without looking up. "I went easy on the drink. I covered the places you said. It was a nerve-wracking business. When I got back I needed something to relax with. I overdid it. I'm sorry I took your liquor; but I'll pay for it—"

Patrick had grabbed him by the shoulders and pulled him to his feet. "You said you went out. You did the round. You came back and drank too much. So you settled on my bed. Is that it?"

"Sure, that's it Ted."

Patrick pushed back against the bed so that he slumped against the wall. "Then I suppose someone came in and cleaned your shoes while you were in a drunken stupor? Look at them." Patrick leaned over him and pulled his head down towards his shoes. "Not a mark on them. You don't know it's rained a bit since I left here yesterday. You don't know it, because you haven't stirred. You started drinking yourself silly soon as my back was turned. You never left the place. Isn't that it?"

Price sat hunched over his knees. He didn't say anything.

Patrick hooked his hand under his chin and dragged his face up as if he would snap his neck. "You never set foot outside the door. That's it, isn't it, you drunken pig?"

Price's face was a ghastly, greenish pallor.

"Yes," he muttered sheepishly.

Patrick's grip tightened as the surge of fury swept through him. His other hand slid round Price's throat. His head throbbed as he told himself that he was trapped. His whole plan had fallen to pieces. He'd relied on this weak drunken moron and ditched himself.

He suddenly realized he was still shaking Price. And Price was trying to say something, but he did not release his grip and the two men lurched across the bed, Patrick's hands clawing at the other's throat.

"You bloody washout," he was babbling in his insensate rage. "You've bust my alibi wide open."

Twenty-Two

Patrick went into the living-room, his legs feeling weak and trembling uncontrollably.

The shock of Price letting him down had been devastating, and now the realization that his attack on the drunken fool couldn't put the mess right only increased his desperate state of mind.

In his fury he'd nearly strangled Price. He pushed a hand wearily across his sweating face, thankful that he'd come to his senses in time and had let Price go. It was a crazy thing to have done, anyway. It would turn the fool against him, that's all it would do. It was crazy of him to allow his temper to ride. The problem demanded cool consideration. A bit of time and a clear head.

He plunged his shaking hands into his pockets. He'd got to go careful. Careful with Price. The man could do him even more harm than he'd done already. If he heard about the raid and the dead copper. Price might scare. He'd certainly string things together and take Patrick for a murderer. Price could spill the whole damned business to the gendarmes.

He'd got to make things up with Price. He'd got to soften up a bit himself. Explain the position Price had dropped him into. But point out it was all over and done with now and no anger or argument could change it. They'd got to find another alibi between them, somehow. That was the line to take. He'd got to get the moron back on his side. It wasn't going to be easy after all the rough stuff; but Patrick couldn't send him away smarting with revenge.

Patrick forced himself to keep calm, to use a clear head. He'd got to square things with Price, and find a new alibi.

Without looking through the partly-opened curtains, beyond which he'd left the other sprawling on the bed, he went into the kitchen, sticking his hat on a peg behind the living-room door. He turned the key in the door and then he bent down at the cupboard under the sink. Inside were saucepans, a box of soap-powder and odds and ends of cleaning materials.

He took the lid off the largest of the saucepans at the back of the cupboard and carefully transferred the loot from his pocket into it. He pushed pieces of newspaper round the glittering, gleaming stuff so that it wouldn't rattle if the saucepan was knocked and fitted the lid snugly back. He closed the cupboard door and took off his raincoat and hung it on the peg under his hat. He unlocked the door and went back into the living-room.

Price had pulled himself together sufficiently to get off the bed and now he was standing by the sitting-room window looking out at the rain. He'd changed into his own clothes and combed his hair, but the stubble was coming through on his chin. He glanced sheepishly over his shoulder at Patrick.

"I deserved all I got, Ted," he said morosely. "Damned sorry I let you down. I just went haywire when I got the booze in me." He took his hand out of his jacket pocket and crossed to the table. He put down five one pound notes. "I reckon I owe you more than that," he said. "But it's all I can do at the moment. Return the fiver."

"Put them back in your pocket," Patrick said quietly. "We all fall down on a job once in a while. It's just one of those things. Squabbling won't help. We've got to get together and work out something else."

Price's expression brightened. He picked up the money, folding the notes slowly before slipping them back into his pocket.

"Okay, Ted," he said hopefully. "And no hard feelings?"

"Hard feelings won't help, Harry. Let's cut the losses and start again. Sit down."

Price sat down gingerly, his hand going to his head and his face a grimace of pain, as he did so. "My head feels like it's between a steam-hammer and an anvil."

Patrick didn't say anything. He sat on the edge of the table and pulled out a packet of cigarettes.

"A cig might help," he suggested, offering the packet; but Price recoiled at the thought of it.

"I'd sooner have a couple of aspirins, Ted, if you've got such a thing."

"Should be some." Patrick slid off the table and went to the bathroom.

It seemed a crazy notion to be trying to fix the headache of a flop who'd just let him down; but he had to make sure Price kept his mouth shut The treatment was working. It was easier than he'd expected. He'd got him on his side, and by telling him to stick to the fiver, he'd got him eating out of his hand.

Now he'd got to think up a new alibi. He felt pretty sure Price wouldn't have any bright suggestions. The drink hadn't completely worked off yet. He'd just have to get him shipshape then bung him off, so that he could concentrate on his own.

The bathroom was very small. Not much bigger than the bath. But there was room for the small cupboard on the wall. There was a shaving mirror in the door and inside a couple of shelves. On the lower one was his shaving-brush, razor, toothbrushes and paste. The upper one contained some medicine bottles, a tin of sticking-plaster and a couple of boxes of ancient pills. There was a packet of aspirins, too, and as he rummaged to find them at the back of the shelf he disturbed one or two of the bottles. The doctor's name was on the bottles. The mixtures were made up at the doctor's own dispensary.

He stood for a moment, holding up one of the bottles staring vaguely at the doctor's name.

He began to think of the doctor's waiting-room. Out of the blue it struck him that if only he'd been waiting to see the doctor he couldn't be elsewhere. Abstractedly the thought carried on that he had the germ of an alibi, but he shrugged it off. It was too crazy to contemplate. For a start, his doctor wouldn't play and besides, an hour in a waiting-room and surgery, even if he could somehow get his doctor to agree to the idea, which he knew was fantastic, wouldn't cover him for his visit to the house, and the cop's death early that morning.

He put the bottle back and took the aspirins, but he still couldn't shake off the idea. He was scowling to himself, and he suddenly thought there was something in it, if he could find the right doctor. Which was when he thought of Steiner.

And then Ted Patrick was confident he had the answer. He had his alibi.

He splashed some water in a tumbler and went back to Price. Now he'd got the idea all he wanted was to get rid of Price and set to work. He handed over the aspirin tablets and the glass of water and stood dragging at a fresh cigarette. Price swallowed the aspirins gratefully and gulped down some water.

"Hope that does the trick," he said. "Thanks, Ted."

Patrick nodded and smiled with what he hoped looked like

sympathy. "You still look a bit pale about the gills," he said. "If I were you I'd get back to your place and take it easy for a while. I know how wicked a hangover is. You need a bit of time to work them off."

The other looked up at him over the glass in faint surprise.

"But what about you? I've dropped you in the cart. Least I can do is try and help you out."

Patrick shook his head. He hoped he was putting on a benevolent expression.

"You're not to worry, Harry. It won't help the hangover. I'll work something out. I'll let you know if I need your help."

Price got up. He had a moment of unsteadiness which convinced him that Patrick was right about him getting back to his own place for a long lie-down. "If that suits you." The relief was plain in his face. "I'll take your advice. I feel lousy." He moved slowly over to the door. "You're sure I can't do anything?"

"I'll manage," Patrick said, joining him at the top of the short staircase. He was about to produce a ten-shilling note and tell him to get himself a taxi, then he decided he would be overdoing it and might arouse Price's suspicion that he wanted to get rid of him. He watched him go out of the lower door into the mews.

Patrick turned back into the room and lit another cigarette from the stub of the old one. Then he picked up the telephone directory and turned to the S's. He remembered Steiner all right, but it was more than a year since he'd had any dealings with him. He needed to confirm if he still had his dump in Maida Vale.

Dr. Steiner was a naturalized British subject. He'd come to England from Hamburg way back. He'd made a lot of money out of medicine, most of it, Patrick knew, came from its less lawful practices. His so-called consulting-rooms were in Maida Vale, but he ran a small nursing-home near Elstree. Not much more than a dozen beds, but the patients had to pay a packet to get one. Patrick knew the kind of patients they were. Some of them were crazy for a cocaine or heroin kick, some were rich, pregnant girls, who stayed a night or two and came away minus what they'd gone in with and anything from seventy-five pounds to a hundred-and-fifty. Cash.

Patrick knew of the doctor's discreet activities, but Steiner was always able to cover up the more profitable work. His ordinary patients spoke highly of his ability and qualifications, which gave him a good surface reputation.

Patrick always investigated anyone he contemplated working for, just to be certain he wouldn't be swindled out of his cut. He'd dug up all the dirt on Steiner before undertaking a little smuggling assignment for him.

It had been a small job, but there'd been a big risk. Bringing dope back from the Continent after meeting Steiner's contact in Marseilles. Paying a visit to Steiner a couple of days after landing, and exchanging two or three packages for a bundle of crisp fivers.

Patrick didn't like dealing in dope, but that was a time when he'd been glad to deal in anything to pick up a bit of cash.

Patrick didn't fancy the man. Too suave; cold with a sadistic glint in his eyes. He didn't know how the poor dope-ridden types, the others who went to his nursing-home could let him maul them. He thought they must be desperate.

Like he was now.

He found Steiner's name. He was still operating from Archer Crescent. He made a note of the number, but he didn't bother with the telephone. He wasn't going to make an appointment. Just drop in. He thought Steiner would remember him, and see him. Patrick didn't think there'd be any difficulty about having a talk.

He wondered the best line to take. He wouldn't want to say too much. Just tell him he needed an alibi. All Steiner would need to do was simply confirm that Patrick had been admitted to his nursing-home for a very minor operation. He'd entered the home yesterday afternoon, the op had been performed last night and he had been allowed to leave after lunch to-day. What could be simpler? There was no risk for Steiner. His small nursing-home staff were paid to support him in everything he did and said. No matter what.

Patrick thought he had a good approach. He'd point out that one good turn deserved another and he'd remind Steiner of the last occasion they were in touch. Even so, he was still willing to buy his alibi. He didn't think the doctor would be awkward; but if he tried anything, there was always blackmail.

He could bust the doctor's practice wide open if he wasn't

going to co-operate. He felt pretty sure that Steiner woud think twice before refusing such a small favour. After all, it wouldn't help him to be struck off. Even Steiner wouldn't enjoy the thought of that.

The more Patrick considered the proposition the more he knew he had a winner. It was a damned sight better alibi than the one he'd worked out with Price. He wished like hell he'd thought of it before. To be in a nursing-home at the time of the actual crime with the doctor and nursing staff supporting his statement was a cast iron alibi that no one could break.

He eyed his watch. It was pushing one-thirty. Patrick thought if he left in the next few minutes he'd time his arrival towards the end of Steiner's lunch-break. That would be just right. The man was likely to be more affable. Lunch had a way of mellowing people; or maybe it just made them sleepy so they couldn't be bothered to make the effort to be aggressive.

He put on his coat and hat, locked up the flat, and went out into the light drizzle, making his way towards the Edgware Road.

Twenty-Three

Archer Crescent was a short road close to the borders of Maida Vale and St. John's Wood. It was a quiet backwater with prim, dignified houses that had at one time employed half a dozen servants to keep them that way. Now some of the properties had been adapted to meet the requirements of less opulent days, and had been converted into flats and apartments. But the facade had been retained so that the street hadn't lost its original atmosphere in which had glittered the Victorian gas lamps and clop-clopping broughams.

On one side was a block of terraced houses close to the pavement. Opposite were houses which stood detached, each in its own bit of ground. These houses were further back, too, and had a patch of garden with flowering shrubs and trees, enclosed by hedges. Most of them had a wide single gate and a gravel drive to the garage. One of these belonged to Dr. Steiner.

Patrick paused outside the gate, taking in the place. It was a three-storey house with the small windows at the top looking out from attics. On the first and ground floors the windows were the long sash type, discreetly covered by white net curtains. The porch projected from the wide, heavy front-door and a couple of steps stretched up to it. On the same side as the garage and between it and the house was a low wing with a door centre. A brass plate at the side denoted that here was the consulting room. Patrick remembered it all very clearly; but he didn't remember the sleek car standing outside the garage.

He walked across to the front door admiring the car. It was an Alvis. Three-litre job with the body by Graber of Switzerland. He thought it must have set Steiner back a cool three thousand or more. He was glad to know that Steiner was still doing nicely. It gave Patrick his trump card if he should prove difficult. The doctor wouldn't want to place all his wordly goods in jeopardy for the sake of covering up a pal.

He pushed the bell at the side of the front-door. He reckoned most callers would be by appointment, the girls in trouble and the drug-addicts being very private. He didn't think the side door was used much.

His eyes dwelt on the long cream bonnet of the Alvis. With what he'd got in the kitchen cupboard he could do much better than that. Provided there was no trouble; so long as the gendarmes didn't come sniffing around, he'd eventually be able to cash it and live in a style as grand as Steiner. And there wasn't going to be any trouble.

He felt a surge of confidence that he could fix it now; that Steiner would play along. After all, there wasn't such a great difference between the way they made the cash. The results were the same if the methods were different. It was just that Steiner was less likely to get caught. Nobody chased him. He belonged to a respectable profession and put up a respectable facade. Nobody thought of trying to chip away the edges and look underneath.

His mind drifted to Harry Price. He'd have to be taken care of over this. Patrick was speculating on how to make sure that the other wouldn't blab about the arrangement they'd had, and how he'd got drunk and ruined it. It was only the fool's word against his, he decided; and if it came to anything the fact that he'd admittedly passed out into a drunken coma for who knows how many hours would go against him. All the same Patrick was wishing he'd had enough foresight to have got Price, out cold as he was, out of his flat and dumped him. Back at his own joint, for example. Then he could have bluffed the other that the whole thing had been a product of his drunken imagination.

Patrick was still worrying the problem when a youngish woman opened the door.

"Dr. Steiner at home?"

She looked at him doubtfully. He could tell she was wondering what he was doing there, obviously without an appointment.

"He has a patient at the moment."

"So now he's got himself two." Patrick leered at her. She was one of Steiner's fixtures he hadn't seen before. Perhaps he had to switch his secretaries pretty frequently.

"Have you an appointment?" she said. She made it sound polite, but she wasn't holding the door wide enough to make it look like a welcome.

He shook his head. "But he won't mind that. We've worked together before."

The girl stepped back, faintly surprised, and Patrick moved into the hall. "What name?"

"Patrick."

"Dr. Patrick?"

"If it gives you any joy." He smiled at her, following her into a large high-ceilinged room.

"Would you mind waiting?" she said, and went out, closing the door.

He lit a cigarette and looked around appreciatively. There was a large oak table in the centre of the room. The carpet was dark patterned, sumptuous to walk on. There was a three-seater settee and a couple of arm-chairs to match its tawny upholstery. Chairs were evenly spaced around the table and bookcases with attractively glazed doors filled the recesses either side of the fire-place in which a coal fire glowed. The chandelier was old-fashioned but elaborate, and the only note of modernity was a tall standard lamp with an inverted bowl designed to splash the bulb's glare at the ceiling.

It was a comfortable room, but there was a stuffiness about it, as if it needed a lot of fresh air. The windows were latched tight shut, Patrick noted. There were three or four glossy magazines on the table, but no ashtrays. The inference was obvious, but he was in no mood to appreciate the interpretation.

He put his hat and raincoat on a chair and stood near the fire dragging at his cigarette. The house was quiet. He saw the pair of slender, expensive-looking gloves left lying half-beneath a cushion in one of the arm-chairs. So the patient was a woman.

Patrick grinned. Naturally, she was one of Steiner's patients. A faint whiff of scent clung to the atmosphere, and he hoped she'd come back for them while he was there. He was curious to see the kind of number she was.

He'd just flicked the end of his cigarette into the fire when the door opened and an attractive young woman came in. She carried a neatly-rolled umbrella, and when she saw Patrick she pulled her fur-coat around her, but not so quick that he didn't glimpse her figure. Her face would have been even prettier if it hadn't been for the pale, drawn look. She had all the tell-tale signs that brought a rich and attractive young woman to Steiner. He moved quickly forward and picked up the gloves.

"You looking for these?"

"Thank you," she said in a debutante voice. He noticed that she wore no rings on her fingers, and he could see she was in a hurry to go.

She turned back to the door as the youngish woman came in briskly, to glance at Patrick with a sudden frown removing her professional smile.

"So sorry, madam," she said. "I could have got those for you." He grinned to himself as the door closed on the patient and Dr. Steiner's secretary. Steiner hadn't dropped the illegal side of business, not by the look of it.

It was two or three minutes later that the secretary came back and said the doctor would see him, and Patrick followed her along the hall and he was shown into a room he only vaguely remembered.

It was plainly furnished. A large flat-topped writing-desk, a bookcase at the back along the wall, a deep leather arm-chair, and a straight-backed soft-seated chair with arms, in front of the desk. A cabinet and almost hidden by it, a washbasin, and a high, hard medical couch with a large anglepoise lamp on a small table beside it.

A dark plain folding-screen stood on one side of the room, and Patrick found himself picturing the feminine patients undressing behind it.

He gave his attention to the figure eyeing him from the writing-desk.

Twenty-Four

Steiner was in his middle forties. He had a thin patch of fair hair greased flat on his scalp, a style that emphasized the width and depth of his forehead. His features were heavy, but he had a suave manner that probably helped at the bedside, and he spoke with only the faintest trace of foreign accent.

Steiner nodded to the young woman who had waited expectantly, and she went out, closing the door quietly.

"What can I do for you?" Steiner said pleasantly to Patrick. He indicated a chair and the other lounged in it casually.

"You remember me?"

Steiner put his elbows on the leather arms of his swivel chair, and gently stroked his long, bulbous nose. He looked as if he was thinking hard.

"You came for a consultation about a year or eighteen months ago. Is that not so?"

Patrick leaned back, a faint grin on his face.

"Not quite," he said pleasantly. "You'll have to check your records. I'll save you the trouble. I came here on a little assignment for you, I'd just returned from Marseilles. I'd met a friend of yours there."

"That is very interesting, but I do not see what bearing it has on your presence here now."

"I'm coming to that," Patrick said in the same friendly tones. "I just wanted to remind you of how we last met."

"Proceed please," Steiner said.

"Your friend gave me one or two small items which I delivered to you," Patrick said. "You will remember how important the small items were."

Steiner continued to stroke his nose, his eyes had half-closed, but he didn't stop looking at Patrick.

"You will forgive me, but I have a poor memory perhaps; but are you sure you have come to the right address?"

Patrick had expected Steiner to be a bit cautious at the beginning. He continued to keep his tone on a friendly, sociable level. "Still got your little nursing-home outside Elstree?"

Steiner nodded slowly.

"I have a nursing-home there, yes. But I do not understand how this can concern you."

Patrick leaned forward; his voice hardened. "Let me put it this way. I helped you out at no small risk to myself. You were grateful. Now it's my turn, I'm the one who needs a little help. Just a small favour requiring nothing more than a receipt."

Steiner frowned, obviously undecided. He didn't know whether the best line was to admit their previous association or to go on faking ignorance.

"This is a very curious discussion," he said at length. "I am sure there is some misunderstanding. I cannot recall any transaction I have had with you. However," a suggestion of a smile curled the corners of his mouth, "if I can help an old patient in distress, I will do what I can."

Patrick restrained himself from trying to call the other's bluff; he knew the best way to get results was to keep it relaxed. "It's not a hand-out I want," he said easily. "I want an alibi."

Steiner remained unruffled. There was not a glimmer of surprise or any other emotion in his face.

"I prescribe treatment for physical ills, not social," he said quietly. "I do not know what trouble you have got into and I do not wish to know; but I cannot be a party to it."

"There's nothing to it. And it's simple for you." Patrick heard his voice waver slightly, and he continued more calmly. "All you have to do is give me a receipt for treatment in your nursing-home during the last twenty-four hours. Just to show I was admitted yesterday afternoon and discharged to-day."

"Such a procedure does not appear all that simple to me," Steiner said. "You expect me to perpetrate some sort of crime in order to extricate you from another crime?" He spread his hands helplessly. "Why come to me? You need a lawyer."

"I want an alibi," Patrick said, keeping his rising fury in check. "You can give it me with a stroke of the pen. I can tell you why it's necessary. There's been an accident. The police'll question me—I——"

"I can quite understand why alibis are necessary," Steiner interrupted him coldly. "I do not wish to hear the reason for yours. Whatever it is, my answer is the same. I am sorry, but I can do nothing."

Patrick eyed the other steadily. There was still the last

card to play. He'd got to play it calmly. The easier he put it across the better the result.

"You trying to set yourself up as something you know you're not, Doc?" he said. "Trying to kid me that doing me this little favour would be out of character? As if I didn't know that the consignment I smuggled over for you was for the addicts you've got on your list. As if I didn't know about the wealthy young women you keep out of the gossip columns. I just met one of them in your waiting-room. Nice girl she looked. Unmarried. I don't doubt she'll pay well. I'd be willing to pay myself. Now, wouldn't you like to think over my little request?"

Apart from the tightening of his mouth Steiner's expression hadn't changed. He said, his accent a little thicker: "I do not require to think it over, even when you threaten blackmail." His fingers drummed on the desk. "I do not think there is any more to say."

"I haven't finished yet," Patrick shot at him, leaning forward, his hands gripping the arms of the chair. "I can break you. A few hints in the right quarters would bring the cops round you like flies, poking their noses into that little nursing-home, for instance." His voice rose. "You'd lose everything you've got, Steiner, and you know it. Wouldn't that be a pretty big sacrifice for the sake of a piece of paper?"

"Blackmail requires a blackmailee as well as the blackmailer," Steiner said without anger. "You have picked the wrong person for the former role. Now, you have come here and talked a lot of nonsense, but I am willing to forget it if you will leave me."

Patrick sat tensed, frustrated desperation choking him. He'd got to make the other see it his way.

"So you're going to take what's coming to you?" he said. "You're prepared to let me blow the gaff, rather than put your damned name on a receipt?"

"It rather depends how foolish you are," Steiner said suavely. "It would be your word against mine, and I am a doctor. A respected member of my profession. You are a criminal, known to the police, who has now got yourself in more trouble."

"Even if they doubt my word," Patrick snarled impotently, "I'll set them probing."

The other shrugged. "As you wish," he said. "But if you are sensible you will keep your mouth shut. And I will forget this unpleasant interview." He pressed a bell on his desk and almost immediately the door opened.

Patrick swung round expecting to see the young woman. Instead, the heavy figure of a man in a white coat stood there.

Steiner turned to the man at the door, smiling faintly.

"Would you show the patient out," he said.

All the way back from Archer Crescent Ted Patrick kept telling himself he was licked. He was scared, at his wits' end; and at the same time he boiled with fury when he thought of the patience and care with which he'd planned the job.

It had come to nothing. Everything had gone wrong. The dead copper. The alibi, that drunken flop, Price. And now Steiner.

Ted Patrick climbed the stairs to his flat with a heavy tread. He knew Sterner was right. Steiner knew he was bluffing. He knew he wouldn't go to the police. What good would it do him when the busies came for him to up and spout about Dr. Steiner's little caper? They wouldn't be interested in what he had to say about Steiner; the only thing they'd be interested in would be what he had to say about the dead cop on the Hickham Road and Hull's missing sparklers.

Steiner knew he'd been safe to tell him to go to hell.

The afternoon editions of the evening papers were full of it. Patrick threw the paper he'd bought on to the table and poured himself the last dregs from the gin-bottle. He tried to get some comfort from his drink, but every drop was sour in his mouth.

Things had moved fast, according to the paper. The body had been found; some farmer, out on an early morning pigeon-shoot along the plantation, had stumbled on it. They'd traced it back through the hedge to the spot in the road, which had already been scraped for bloodstains by the forensic boys. The glass splinters had been picked up, too, and a preliminary examination of the injuries suggested that the cop had been run down by a car.

They weren't wasting much time.

Already the damned gendarmes were linking the corpse with the jewel-robbery at nearby Hickham Hall, home of the well-known sportsman, Jimmy Hull. They were also searching the area for the stolen car. The service-station assistant at the garage on Eastern Avenue had come forward to report that a man had approached as he was closing up the previous night and had bought an ignition-key for a Vauxhall.

The service-station chap remembered the series letters which were the same as on the ignition-lock of the model stolen from the *Spinning Wheel* car park. He had gone on to describe how the stranger had arrived on foot just as he had locked the office and had offered the excuse of having left his keys in his car which he had locked up without thinking. The garage lights were out, the man said and the stranger had worn his coat-collar turned up and his snap-brim hat pulled down over his eyes. He had remained in the shadows so the assistant was unable to give any description, but the other had tipped him generously.

And he wasn't the only witness reported in the newspaper. Another garage attendant at Chelmsford had volunteered the information that late the same night he had served a man with petrol who'd remained seated in his car and gave the impression he was trying to conceal his appearance as much as possible. His coat-collar was high and his hat brim low. He had ordered his tank to be filled up.

The car was a black Vauxhall with the same registration letters as that of the stolen car, but, of course, the attendant hadn't taken any particular interest at the time, and didn't know the registration number.

All this stuff was being followed up and had led the police into suspecting the stolen car had been used for the robbery and the killing of the cop. Scotland Yard had been called in, the newspaper said, detectives led by Inspector Hood were on the job.

Patrick knew Hood. Hood knew him. Patrick finished his drink. Whatever they picked up in Suffolk, and he was confident Myra would give nothing away, they would get on to him before very long. Hood would be along, asking him chattily where he'd spent yesterday and last night and this morning. Waiting for him to prove the answers. Patrick knew the old routine. He'd be a suspect until he could prove his alibi. And he hadn't got an alibi to prove.

He stared moodily at the headlines. He'd have to do something about the loot. He couldn't keep it in the flat. There'd be a search-warrant eventually if he couldn't find an alibi. The place would be turned upside down. There was no safe spot to hide it on the premises. He'd have to think of something.

But first of all he'd have to think up an alibi. That was more important right now.

He idly turned the pages of the paper, in case there was any other stuff referring to the caper he'd pulled, and which had gone so cross-eyed on him. He might have missed something during his first panicky run-through.

But there was nothing more than the headlines and story on the front page. He kept turning over the pages trying desperately to dream up an idea for a damned alibi and cursing luridly aloud.

Twenty-Five

The place reminded Dr. Morelle of the offices of the Detective Division at the Palais de Justice at Lyons. And his mind went back to his experiences there when he had worked with the great detective, and close friend, the late Harry Sodermann. As he paced up and down the office Dr. Morelle was describing to Miss Frayle some of the adventures that had come his way in those far-off days. Miss Frayle was more interested in the project at hand, but she did her best to appear interested in Dr. Morelle's reminiscences.

The Palais of Justice, he was explaining now, was a huge building with an enormous flight of steps running down toward the river. But the Detective Division was at the back of the vast building and was the reverse of imposing, it was reached by a narrow side street and in the entrance, beyond the doorway, stood a venerable switchboard, run by an old detective with gout. Beyond him the narrow corridor led to the jail.

Dr. Morelle drew on his inevitable Le Sphinx as he recalled the office off this corridor, large, indescribably dusty and crowded with ancient filing-cabinets, a kind of giant memory. French police-files were supposed to be the most thorough in the world. The files at Lyons were encyclopaedic and must have weighed countless tons. Anyone who had ever come to the attention of the police had a dossier, each containing all the information available on its subject, and kept up-to-date by additional items supplied by detectives, which might turn out to be useful at some future date.

The laboratory was three storeys above the office, reached by a winding staircase. "One morning," Dr. Morelle said, "I got there early, just as the door swung open and in came the jailer, followed by a motley collection of prisoners, and after them followed the great Sodermann himself. I had by now learned that the popular conception of the romantic scoundrel or dashing criminal was nothing but a myth; Lyons was a city of about a million inhabitants, the night's police haul was always twenty or thirty. On this particular morning one of the prisoners appeared to be a well-to-do middle-class business man, who answered Sodermann's questions politely.

"For what crime are you here?" Sodermann asked this man.

'The man answered perfectly calmly. 'I killed my wife last evening'."

"Oh," Miss Frayle said, and Dr. Morelle smiled thinly at her shocked expression.

"It was not my business to ask," he went on, "but the question slipped out. Why? I asked the man."

"Even more coolly he replied: 'I have been thinking for twenty years of doing it.' I remember how Harry Sodermann remained completely unmoved and went on filling out the man's record, but those emotionless words provided me with a glimpse of that dark abyss into which my life has often since compelled me to look."

"Poor man," Miss Frayle said. "The man who killed his wife, I mean. Not you, of course, Dr. Morelle."

"Of course, Miss Frayle."

The building selected as the venue for the offices of the committee that had been set up under Dr. Morelle's direction for the investigation of witness's evidence, and which reminded him of his days with the Lyons Detective Division, was an old-fashioned office-block overlooking the Edgware Road end of Marylebone Road.

The offices occupied a first floor suite which was reached by a wide stairway, particularly convenient to take the flow of people who, it was anticipated, were likely to call in response to the appeal made especially to them.

The committee had followed the example of the French experiment, and which Dr. Morelle, after collecting all the information he could from Paris, had decided would be equally appropriate for London. The scheme was simple to operate, required nothing more than an office for interviews, and a shorthand-typist to take down statements.

As soon as the committee was in being, the scheme had been devised in detail, a street chosen and a newspaper advertisement drafted. Tuesday had been decided as the first day for the experiment.

That the response had been beyond expectation had not surprised Dr. Morelle. He knew to what lengths some individuals would go to claim attention, revelling in self-importance as they aired what they thought was their special knowledge in the limelight of the public stage, the type of witness who was unreliable, always identifying himself or herself with some sensational case in which the part played was more fiction than truth.

Of course, this type was far outnumbered by witnesses at trials or in the coroner's courts who were not sensation-mongers or publicity-seekers; indeed, they would prefer to remain unseen in the background, and they came forward as dutiful citizens endeavouring to help the community. But even their observations were coloured, inhibited by all the irrelevant trimmings. One of Dr. Morelle's purposes in carrying out the investigation, was to try and discover what mental aberration prompted this peculiar characteristic in otherwise normal individuals.

He had not been surprised so much by the weight of the response from those purporting to have been in Half Moon Street at a quarter-past-six that Tuesday morning, and who maintained they had actually witnessed the accident referred to in the evening newspapers, each with his or her own colourful account of the scene. Some described the elderly man who had been knocked down, others named the company who owned the vehicle responsible; many insisted that the ambulance was a long time coming. Descriptions were graphic and detailed, and everyone was different.

If it did nothing else the experiment was demonstrating the fallibility of human beings. So many were obviously sincere and believed themselves to have seen what had never actually taken place. Dr. Morelle wished that having gained Inspector Hood's interest in the experiment, that it should have coincided with a case to which his old friend had been suddenly assigned. He would have found the investigation as enlightening as Gerald Winterton and the other members of the committee who had won the cooperation of the witnesses.

Dr. Morelle had noted the quiet enthusiasm with which Miss Frayle was carrying out her work. When the scheme was first proposed he had fancied she had been sceptical, although he was aware that she was too respectful and conscientious to voice her criticism of any activity he undertook.

She had taken over the organization of the interviews, acted as receptionist and was never flustered by the callers bustling into the outside office which was used as a waiting-room. At the same time, she managed to cope with the special points he wanted noted and recorded.

By four o'clock that afternoon the committee had received some forty-five callers. The men had outnumbered the women by two to one, but each one of them had given a different description of an imaginary event, many of them with a force and confidence that sometimes even the members of the committee would admit to wondering if the accident had in fact taken place. Each interview had varied in duration from two to four minutes, and the committee, the stenographer and Miss Frayle had been kept going continuously without a break.

A few minutes after four the pressure eased and for the first time that afternoon the waiting-room was empty. Dr. Morelle turned to the three committee-members, besides Winterton, named Hargreaves, Owen and Dutton, rose from his chair at the table and moved over to the window, stretching his cramped leg muscles. His hooded eyes flickered momentarily over the passing traffic in the street below, then slowly came to bear on his companions. Hargreaves was an eminent sociological writer, Owen a distinguished lawyer and magistrate, and Dutton was head of St. Pat's Hospital psychological department.

"You have seen something of the mental aberrations peculiar even in the most normal individuals, demonstrated this afternoon," he said. "Not one of our callers could tell us the truth. Not one of them suggested that nothing had taken place in Half Moon Street this morning. We know from our cross-examination that at most only fifty per cent were in the vicinity at that time. How did any of them come to believe in their story? Can we ascribe it entirely to the subconscious suggestion invoked by our advertisement?" He came back to the table, holding out his thin gold cigarette-case.

Hargreaves and Owen got slowly to their feet.

When his cigarette was alight, Hargreaves said thoughtfully:

"Most extraordinary. In all my experience, I should not have believed that so many would come forward and not one be able to speak the truth."

"I don't think the result was so very much different in

France," Owen said. "I think, as you suggested, Dr. Morelle, many people automatically accept an idea because it is described authoritively as having taken place."

Winterton nodded in agreement, and Dutton murmured appropriately. Dr. Morelle's enigmatic expression barely concealed the pleasure he derived from the realization of the most useful findings which the experiment was going to produce.

"That would appear to be the most obvious theory," he said to Owen. "Once a situation has been suitably planted, it would seem there are any number of normal individuals who feel themselves identified with it and who are ready to swear they had witnessed the scene."

"Nevertheless," Hargreaves murmured, his mature, long-jawed face reflecting incredulity. "You would have expected one sensible, down-to-earth person among them who, if he had really been there at the time stated this morning, would have insisted on giving us a true picture?"

Winterton had stood up and was about to say something as by way of an answer, when Miss Frayle came into the room from the outer office, and Dr. Morelle glanced at her speculatively.

"I thought you might like to take advantage of the lull with a little refreshment," Miss Frayle said. "I've had tea sent up."

A faint smile of appreciation touched the corners of Dr. Morellie's mouth. "Most thoughtful of you. Are you looking after yourself?"

"Thank you," Miss Frayle said, more than a little surprised at this unusual consideration on Dr. Morellie's part for her welfare. He was glancing at the others.

"I think we might profitably continue our deliberations over a cup of tea," he said and he turned to Miss Frayle. "We shall close the proceedings for the day at half past five. There may be a few more callers between now and then."

"Very well, Dr. Morelle," Miss Frayle said and hurried out of the room. She was back within a few moments, without the expected tray of tea. "There's another just arrived," she said. "Shall I ask him to wait, while you have your tea first?"

"I think so," Dr. Morelle nodded. "It's a man, is it?"

"Yes," Miss Frayle said, "a Mr. Patrick is the name."

Twenty-Six

Did You See The Accident? the advertisement in the Personal Column ran and continued in small type *An accident occurred at 6:15 this morning at the Picadilly end of Half Moon Street, when an elderly man was knocked down by a tradesman's van. Would anyone who saw the accident please contact the Accident Investigation Committee.*

The address and telephone number were given and Patrick had read the advertisement through again, more slowly. He was sure he'd seen something like this before. He was scowling to himself. There was something fishy about it. If there had been an accident, he was reasoning witnesses would be requested to get in touch with the police, not some committee.

If there'd been an accident. The thought stuck in his mind. And then he realized why. The set-up rang a bell He'd heard about some caper that had taken place in France. Paris, wasn't it? A year or so back. And it was fake. The whole idea as he remembered it was for some bunch of busy-bodies who'd got nothing better to do, to advertise there'd been an accident, an accident that only existed in their minds, and then invite witnesses up for an interview. Kind of crazy idea.

He'd heard that it was surprising the number of fools who'd turned up to report the accident and to give descriptions of what they had seen. Pure imagination, of course He remembered thinking at the time that he couldn't understand why people should go to all that time and money to find out if people were lying. He couldn't see the idea behind the experiment. But it didn't matter. He didn't care.

This could be his alibi.

He read it again and made a note of the address and telephone number. All he had to do was to go along and say that he had been in Half Moon Street at the time stated that morning and tell them there had been no accident.

There'd bound to be a lot of idiots turning up who'd swear they'd seen the old man knocked down. If he insisted that there'd been nothing unusual in Half Moon Street that morning, they'd know he must have been there.

If he was there, and they supported his statement, then he couldn't have been in Suffolk. He couldn't have run down the copper or raided Hickham Hall. This committee lot would have to back him up.

No copper could get round that one.

Patrick pushed his fingers through his hair, his face twisted with self-satisfaction. At last he'd made it. There couldn't be any slips this time. There was no doubt he was right about the set-up. It was the same kind of caper he'd heard about, he was positive of that. As far as he knew it had never been tried out over here before.

He glanced down at the address he'd copied. As the phone number had been included in the ad they obviously invited inquiries on the telephone. He thought it might be an idea to give it a buzz through first, just to get the feel of it.

He dialled the number. After a few moments a girl came on the line and said this was the Accident Investigation Committee.

"Just seen your ad in the evening paper," Patrick said in a matter-of-fact voice. "I was in Half Moon Street at the time of the accident and I'm willing to tell what I saw if it's likely to be any help."

"Thank you for ringing," the girl said. "Would you come round to our office at your earliest convenience?"

"I shall be your way later this afternoon. I could call then."

"We can promise not to keep you long. Could I have your name please——?"

Patrick didn't give his name, but rang off. He lit a cigarette. His spirits rose, confidence flowed back through him. He was all right now.

It was pushing three-thirty. He didn't think it good policy to rush there so soon after fixing it. He stroked his chin pensively. He'd better shave, change his clothes. But before going into the bathroom he looked into the kitchen cupboard. He couldn't resist checking that the loot was safe. Once he'd got the interview over, and his alibi really fixed, and the whole business had died down a bit, he could slip quietly over to Amsterdam and take things real easy.

Fifteen minutes later he was all ready to nip along to this address in Marylebone Road. The rain had stopped and he decided to walk some of the way. He'd get a bus to Marble Arch, down the Edgware Road and cut through. It occurred to him that he'd got to think of a good reason for being in Half Moon Street so early that morning. He'd work something out as he went. It shouldn't be difficult to dream up some plausible reason that would satisfy this bunch of egg-heads. They wouldn't be interested as to why he was there; only in what he had seen. And he'd seen no accident, no tradesman's van knocking down a non-existant old man. He'd seen nothing.

He locked up the flat, walked through the mews, and headed for the Bayswater Road.

When he found the building at the Edgware Road end of Marylebone Road, he thought it looked a pretty crummy sort of set-up, and he was still unimpressed after he climbed the wide staircase up to the first floor and found his way to the office, which was indicated by a temporary cardboard sign. There was a young girl at a typewriter, beating it up, in an outer office, and she took no notice of him as he went through to where another office lay beyond a half-glazed door.

This office, though it was larger than the first one was crummy, too. Worn carpet, cheap inadequate office furniture, except for a big, heavy-looking desk in the corner, beside which a blonde young woman stood, who turned to regard him brightly over horn-rimmed spectacles. She was dealing with a tray of tea-cups and a teapot and milk-jug. She smiled at him a little absently and indicated a chair against the wall.

Ted Patrick grinned back at her and sat down, looking around him and weighing the place up.

Miss Frayle's thoughts had been preoccupied with a mental picture of Dr. Morelle leaving 221B Harley Street at the somewhat unusual hour of six o'clock that morning. As always, she had thought that Dr. Morelle knew best, and had carried out his requests in connection with this accident investigation idea with her usual willingness; but she hadn't been able to arouse much interest when he had asked if she would care to have a look at Half Moon Street at six o'clock the next morning. She preferred her warm bed, and had said so. But she had to confess to herself that her curiosity had been aroused last night when Dr. Morelle had left Harley Street in a hired limousine with a man she had never seen, who had arrived in response to a telephone-call Dr. Morelle had made while she had been out earlier in the day.

She knew it had been something to do with the experiment; but other than that she was in the dark, and Dr. Morelle had not taken the trouble to enlighten her.

That had been late last night and she had forgotten the incident in the rush of business to-day.

She turned her attention to the man who had come into the office and who sat there in his belted raincoat, his hat on his knee, smiling at her quizzically, she thought. Another answer to the advertisement. It had amazed her, the response to the Personal Column item; and the extraordinary inaccurate reports of the supposed witnesses had astounded her even more. She thought it incredible that quite ordinary people could believe the stories they had themselves invented. And she couldn't see any sane reason for it. What peculiar satisfaction did it give them? She decided that although they appeared normal enough on the surface some mental kink must be responsible for their strange reaction to the advertisement.

She sighed and decided that whatever it was, they had provided an interesting lesson in human behaviour, and Dr. Morelle had allowed her yet another insight into the mysterious workings of the human mind.

She finished pouring out the tea and picked up the tray, pausing to ask the man in the raincoat his name before she went into the office where Dr. Morelle was, with the others.

Twenty-Seven

It is most co-operative of you, Mr. Patrick, to volunteer to assist us in our inquiries," Dr. Morelle was saying. "You understand we are anxious to obtain a clear picture of the accident that occurred in Half Moon Street at approximately a quarter-past-six this morning?"

Ted Patrick nodded and smiled confidently at the others round the table who were regarding him with interest. "Only too pleased to help you all I can." This was going to make them look foolish, he was telling himself, and his glance rested on Miss Frayle, who sat at the corner of the table with her notebook.

"Then perhaps you will tell us exactly what you saw happen," Owen said.

Patrick hesitated for a moment. There came the muffled rattle of the typewriter from the outer office, and a taxi hooted in Marylebone Road. Miss Frayle thought that though he was the focus of attention, he showed no sign of nervousness, neither did he appear to be looking for the right thing to say.

"It's pretty simple," Patrick said at length. "I hope you won't misunderstand me. But I was in Half Moon Street at the time you say and I saw nothing happen. Nothing at all."

Hargreaves grunted, Winterton leaned back slowly in his chair, Owen stroked his nose turning to give Dutton a look. Patrick intercepted the glance and was completely confident that he had been right about the set-up from the moment he'd read about it. He could feel himself relax a little. It was all going to be okay.

"You surely must have seen something of the accident if you were there at that time," Dutton said.

"There was nothing," Patrick insisted. "I don't know how and where you got the information; but if there was an accident it didn't happen there at the time you say."

Dr. Morelle was contemplating him with a brooding expression. His gaze shifted to Miss Frayle and back again to Patrick. He said nothing.

"You would be prepared to swear to that?" Hargreaves said.

"Sure thing," Patrick said without hesitation.

"May we ask your occupation?" Owen said, concealing his surprise at the way the interview was going with some difficulty.

"I'm a bit of an actor," Patrick said promptly. "Unemployed, at the moment; in films, that is. Jobs aren't easy to come by."

"And what do you do, if we may ask, in between these jobs?" Gilbert Winterton said.

Patrick gave a shrug. "Odds and ends," he said. "Sometimes I'm lucky on the horses, for instance. Or I do some door-to-door selling. Anything, really. That's honest, of course."

"Quite so," Dr. Morelle said, quietly, and Patrick turned his attention to him. "You must forgive the questions, but they lead to one which I am sure you will appreciate it is necessary to put to everyone. That is, of course, how does it come about that you were in Half Moon Street so early this morning?"

"Simple," Patrick said. "I couldn't sleep. I haven't been getting much work lately and although I try not to show it, it does worry me a bit. About ten days ago I thought I'd landed a part in one of those smaller pictures. Not much, but it was something. Last evening I ran into the agent who'd got me the job, and he told me it was all off. So I went and got a bit plastered. I thought it would stop me worrying and I was hoping for a full night's rest. I woke up at half-past four this morning with a head fit to bust. I just had to get out in the air. And I spent the next couple of hours walking the streets. I wandered round that part of Piccadilly."

He paused and looked round at the faces intent upon him. He grinned faintly at Dr. Morelle, whose expression was smooth and urbane, then Patrick threw Miss Frayle a look. He went on: "I was at the end of Half Moon Street at the time you said in your ad. Naturally, as I hadn't seen any accident, I was puzzled, and thought I'd come along."

"We really are very grateful, Mr. Patrick," Owen said. "And we appreciate the clear and precise manner in which you have given us your observations." He turned to Dr. Morelle and then back to the other. "We cannot go into details, but what you have told us has been of great interest, and will prove an invaluable contribution to our findings in this investigation."

Dr. Morelle gave a nod, apparently in full agreement. "Any further questions," he said to Winterton, Hargreaves and

Dutton, "you would like to put?"

Winterton shook his head.

"No, I don't think so, Dr. Morelle," Hargreaves said slowly.

"I consider Mr. Patrick has covered all the points most adequately," Dutton said, his face glowing with satisfaction.

"Very well," Dr. Morelle said, and his hooded eyes flickered over Patrick's face again. "May we assume you would be available and would be willing to answer any further questions, if that should be necessary?"

Patrick grinned at him. Though this Dr. Morelle, he thought, was a bit of a smoothie, all right. He'd heard about him of course and recognized him at once, from photos in the newspapers. He'd been a bit put out when he realized that Dr. Morelle was mixed up in the malarky, but he wasn't worried now.

"Any time," he said. "You have my address. You've only to get in touch."

"Most kind," Dr. Morelle said. "It only remains for us to thank you for coming along and giving us your co-operation."

There was a murmur of thanks from the others as Patrick stood up and with a faint grin strolled confidently to the door which Miss Frayle had opened for him.

"The first reliable witness we've heard out of the entire lot," Owen said with satisfaction, to Winterton.

"Extremely interesting," Dr. Morelle said, with a thoughtful nod.

Hargreaves was massaging his chin pensively. "Proves one thing," he said. "He was in Half Moon Street this morning, and no mistake."

Patrick had just managed to catch Hargreaves' observation as the door closed behind him and Miss Frayle was accompanying him past the girl beating up the typewriter. In Marylebone Road he allowed the grin of triumph that he had managed to suppress spread now all over his face.

So far as Ted Patrick was concerned, although it had begun raining again and the clouds had banked up, bringing the twilight closer, the skies were blue again. The sunny climate of Mediterranean shores, after a brief business stay in Amsterdam, was just around the corner. There was nothing to ditch him now.

He stopped at a café in the Edgware Road for a meal of ham and chips, washing it down with a pot of tea. The suspense of the interview at the crummy offices he'd left behind him had given him a hell of an appetite. Afterwards he picked up a half-bottle of Scotch at an off-licence and planned a quiet evening celebrating his success alone and working out his next step in the direction of the South of France.

There was no doubt he'd shaken that bunch in their crazy set-up in Marylebone Road. What stuff they'd already heard and how many mugs they had seen, he neither knew nor cared. He knew what he had coughed up had been on the beam. They'd been pretty well impressed. They had no reason to think he should have heard of the experiment before and since he'd given them the facts they must be convinced that he had been there that morning.

Unknowingly, they had given him the safest alibi he had ever had.

Not that the interview had been all plain sailing, although he'd managed to mask his concern successfully. It had been a wise move to go prepared for all kinds of questions. That one about his occupation might have given him a sticky moment if he hadn't already decided to bring in the bit about acting to lead into the worry and insomnia stuff. And the bit about the booze-up was a natural after that, and the insomnia angle had nicely explained his presence in Half Moon Street at the time.

Patrick gave himself up to the luxury dreams of success, as he made his way back to the mews. There was the impression he'd made on that Dr. Morelle character, too, obviously in charge of the set-up. He'd heard he was a mind expert, written books on criminology and that stuff. Helped out the gendarmes at various times, too. Just the sort, in fact, to have on his side in any trouble with the law. With a respected authority like Dr. Morelle supporting his story, his alibi was as safe as the Bank of England.

Soon as he knew he was in the clear, he ruminated, and unlikely to be troubled by the cops, he'd organize his departure. He'd decided he wouldn't just run out on Myra without a word.

She'd be so sick with fury she might spill her story out of revenge. The neat way to handle it was to contact her before he left, tell her he was getting rid of the stuff in Amsterdam, and arrange to meet her in Paris on a date about a fornight later. He fancied she'd fall in with that, because she had agreed that it was unwise to leave Hull too soon, it was likely to arouse suspicion.

So she'd go for any date he suggested, and she'd get to Paris, by which time he'd be in the South of France, or maybe Italy, or Greece; there was no limit to his choice once he'd cashed the goods, so long as it was a place where neither Myra nor the cops could find him.

He turned into the mews, which were dark and shadowed now, with pools of light here and there thrown by electric-lamps in the wall-brackets.

He reached the outside-door to the staircase up to his flat, and then he was halted by a sudden movement in the shadows, and a whisper reached him in familiar tones.

"Oh, Ted... Ted."

Twenty-Eight

When he reached the flat with Myra, the place struck Ted Patrick with a cold, clammy air. He tried to close his mind to it as he bent down and switched on the electric fire. He knew the atmosphere wasn't due to the weather outside. It was Myra's unexpected presence that had sent the temperature down.

He straightened up and looked at her. He hadn't yet recovered from his surprise, and he had to give the impression it was a pleasant surprise.

"Take your coat off, hon," he said. "This place'll soon warm up. Then you can tell me why you've run the risk of coming here."

Myra stared at him, her lower lip trembling.

"Aren't you pleased to see me, Ted?"

"Sure, sure, hon." It was difficult to conceal the irritation in his voice. "But it's not according to plan. Things are pretty sticky and the last thing I wanted was to see you up here so soon."

She took a step forward, loosening her coat, but she didn't take it off. She was wearing a dark dress with a low square neckline. Her blonde hair, ruffled by the wind, fell untidily about her slender throat. Patrick noticed these things half-consciously. He was more conscious of the haunting fear in her eyes.

"Not according to plan, Ted," she whispered. "That's why I had to see you, Ted. Nothing's worked out as we planned."

"What d'you mean?"

"The policeman, you killed him." He saw her knuckles whiten as her fingers pressed into the back of the chair, behind which she was standing. "I couldn't stay at Hickham. Not after the police had been."

"You didn't give anything away?"

"No, Ted; of course not."

"Any of the busies talk to you?"

"A chap from Scotland Yard. Inspector Hood, I think his name was."

"Sure, I know. And I knew you'd get by, honey," Patrick said soothingly.

"But that was before I knew about—about the policeman."

"It was an accident. But what did you tell Hull when you left to-day? Where d'you say you were going?"

"I didn't say anything. I just left."

"That was bright, hon, wasn't it?" he rasped at her. "Now the cops will suspect you've run away."

Myra turned away from him and buried her head in her hands. She was on the verge of hysteria. Patrick tried to collect his reeling senses. He'd got to remain calm. The last person he'd expected to see was Myra and in such a state that would wreck the lucky break that had made his afternoon look bright.

The danger to him now was right here in the flat, and he had to get rid of her. The cops might come nosing around any moment. He had to get her out of his place, but how? He could see she was going to cling like a leech. He'd better start by soothing her down.

He moved to her, putting his arm around her shoulder.

"Dry those peepers while I mix a drink," he said softly. "Then we'll work things out."

She didn't say anything, but dabbed at her eyes with her handkerchief. He went over and poured two slugs of whisky. He didn't add much soda water. He pressed a glass into her hand. He swallowed a mouthful himself and waited for her to drink. She took one sip and pushed the glass on to the table. He pulled out a packet of cigarettes and offered them to her. She shook her head, ignoring the packet and staring at him tensely.

"What are we going to do, Ted?" she demanded.

"Just what we'd arranged to do," he said coolly, taking a deep drag at his cigarette. "You go back to Hickham and carry on as before. You'll have to spin them some story to explain your trip to London. We'll dream up something. I'll hang on here till the thing is off the boil, then breeze over to Amsterdam, cash the sparklers and meet you in Paris as planned."

She was staring at him curiously now.

"Oh, Ted, do you really plan to meet me in Paris?"

"What d'you mean?" He made his tone sound as if he were hurt.

"Had you got around to fixing a place or date?"

He grinned at her disarmingly.

"Time enough for that," he said, "when the job was over. I

was going to get in touch with you before I left so we could fix the details. But we can do it to-night. I just organized myself a cast-iron alibi. I'll have to stay put for a few days till the dust has settled. Then we can move. But you must go back to Hickham pronto, and wait till you hear from me."

"I don't think I could face it alone, Ted. Not after the police-man. Why did you do it——?"

"But there's nothing to connect his death with you or me," he cut in, and it was difficult to keep the snarl of impatience out of his voice. "I told you it was an accident. I never did like vio-lence. The fool stood in the road to hold me up. I couldn't risk stopping. He must have known I'd no intention of obeying his signal. Naturally, I thought he'd jump out of the way."

"They found him off the road, he'd been dragged there." Her tone was hard; she spoke mechanically.

"What else could I do? I couldn't leave him where he was. I went back to see if he was alive." He sighed loudly. "But they can't tie me up with it. Provided you don't give the show away."

He leaned towards her and took her hands. They were like small blocks of ice. All the blood seemed to have drained from them, and there was a grey pallor in her face.

"You must go back, Myra, and play your part. Everything's going to be all right. But you've got to keep your side of the bar-gain. We're in this together, you said. We've got to get out of it together. There's been a hitch, but everything'll straighten out."

"We didn't bargain for a murder," she said.

He gulped in his breath. He could feel the beads of sweat on his forehead. He had a terrifying urge to ram her words down her throat with his fist. Her attitude was driving him crazy. Time was passing and the mess was getting worse. Yet still he fought to retain his patience.

"But I keep telling you," he said slowly, "it was an acci-dent."

"If you run away, they'll call it murder."

"But I'm not running," he insisted. "I'll be here and you'll be there. Then, soon as the heat's eased off, I'll slip off to Amster-dam and a few days later you join me in Paris."

"There'll be more questions, back there," she said. "I know there will. I shall break down. You'll have gone. I can't face it alone. Ted, Ted," she wailed, "don't you see. This makes me an accessory to—to the murder."

Patrick got up, swallowing the remainder of his drink and banged the glass down on the table. He squashed his half-smoked cigarette into an ashtray and lit another. He began to pace about the room. He'd got to do something about her.

If she went back to Hickham he'd be in fear all the time that she'd spill the whole story. He knew that now. And yet she couldn't hang around at the flat. There was nowhere to hide her if anyone called. Besides, if she hadn't returned by the morning Hull would raise the alarm. The cops would put two and two together.

He'd got to get her back to Hickham somehow; but she'd got this damned crazy notion in her head.

"What are we going to do, Ted?"

He paused in front of her. "I've already told you. There's nothing to it, if you go back to-night. And if you just stick to the same story. Repeat what you've already told them. It's as simple as that."

She didn't say anything, just shook her head slowly from side to side. Suddenly she got to her feet. She moved towards the door.

Patrick stepped across and reached the door first. He stood before it, uncertain of her attitude.

"Where you going, Myra?"

"To the police, Ted." Her eyes were wide, her lips trembling. "It's the only way. We've got to tell them. That policeman, he—he's on my conscience. You've got to hand back the stuff. Explain how he died. If you won't, I'll go alone."

"You're crazy," he said thickly. "You'll get us both jailed." She stood her ground, staring at him, blank-eyed.

"You don't want to lose everything we've worked for, hon," he said to her, working all the persuasion he could into his voice. "It's our life together that matters."

"There's no life with a conscience between us," she said. "Let me go, Ted."

His temper flared and he pushed her back against' the wall. She turned back to the telephone on the side-table and snatched the receiver. In one long stride he grabbed at the instrument. He could see her face, twisted with determination before him in a red mist. His hands found the soft flesh of her neck and they tightened. She struggled violently, and all he could see was her white face and her hands clutching for the telephone-receiver which had slipped from her grasp and fallen off the table and swung to and fro on its cord. But he couldn't let go of her throat.

Suddenly she was limp in his arms. Her face was contorted, her eyes staring and glassy. Her tongue was protruding, blackened, between her white teeth, bubbles of froth spumed across her lips.

The sweat poured over Patrick's brow and down the sides of his neck. He saw the swinging telephone. He could hear the dialling tone.

He lowered the body gently to the floor, and reached for the telephone-receiver.

As he placed it back into its cradle, the front-door bell shrilled.

Twenty-Nine

The black Humber, with its tiny light in the centre of the bonnet like a Cyclops eye, moved slowly in the traffic stream crossing Edgware Road into Upper Berkeley Street. It was dark now, and the streets glistened wet in the lights of the ever-increasing traffic flowing east and west. Most of the homeward rush had passed and now Londoners were on their way to begin the evening's entertainment.

Inspector Hood wasn't really aware of his surroundings. Even the slow journey towards Harley Street failed to arouse any impatience with the traffic hold-ups. He sat alone in the back of the car, the blackened bowl of his pipe cold as he gripped its stem in his teeth, characteristic of his reflective mood.

This idea of Dr. Morelle about an experiment to test the unreliability of witnesses. A faked-up situation and an invitation to anyone to come along and report what they had seen. Dr. Morelle had asked him to serve on the committee. He would have accepted but for pressure of work.

He had suggested he would much appreciate being kept informed of the scheme and the results. He readily agreed that the strange statements purporting to be the truth made by some witnesses not infrequently placed Justice in jeopardy, though he'd been a bit dubious about an experiment which invited this type of witness to display his imaginative powers outside the courts, before some unofficial body.

All the same there was no one who held Dr. Morelle in greater respect than Inspector Hood. He had felt certain Dr. Morelle could gain something of use and interest from the experiment. This Ted Patrick business was an example. Dr. Morelle had caught on to him at once, in that uncanny way of his, and had tipped off Scotland Yard. Another of those coincidences which were always cropping up and for which Inspector Hood was forever being grateful. To think that one of the callers, the only one it seemed who had turned out to be an accurate observer, should be none other than Ted Patrick.

Inspector Hood felt very curious about Patrick. Not only was the Hull job just the type that fitted Patrick's *modus operandi,* on a bigger scale, but ever since he'd talked to Mrs. Hull's personal maid that morning, he had felt in the back of his mind that there was a connection somewhere.

Myra Campbell had appeared composed and relaxed enough, and Hull had corroborated that she had been with him at Newmarket from half-past five a.m. until they had returned at about eleven, urging Inspector Hood to refrain from mentioning the matter to Mrs. Hull. But there was something about her which had started a bell ringing faintly at the back of his mind. He couldn't pin it down, but he would.

He'd kept thinking about it at odd moments all day and then there'd been this phone-call from Dr. Morelle which he had received just as he had been about to leave the Hickham police-station to return to London. It was then the penny had dropped. Ted Patrick. He felt certain he had seen the girl with him about a year ago, or maybe a little more, when he had reason to call on that villain in the course of some inquiries he was making. He was pretty sure it was the same girl.

If so, then it would appear to be more than coincidence that she happened to be employed in a house that had been robbed by a thief of Patrick's sort. The method of entry. No damage done, no locks tampered with, no windows removed. Right from the start Inspector Hood had entertained the suspicion it might be an inside job. This Myra Campbell, she could have been on the inside, gone off with Hull, who was obviously cheating on his wife, and left the rest to her boy-friend.

Inspector Hood re-lit his pipe. He was realizing that while Dr. Morelle had sparked the theory, he had at the same time choked it at birth. He could link up the girl with Patrick, but Patrick had a strong alibi. Hadn't Dr. Morelle told him that the crook had described how he was in Half Moon Street the morning of the breaking and entering? So he couldn't have been miles away down in Suffolk. It was impossible to connect him with that job, or the policeman's death.

The police-car had stopped outside 221B Harley Street before Hood realized he was there. He told the sergeant at the wheel not to wait, tapped the ash from his pipe, and reached the door of Dr. Morelle's house. In response to his ring a blonde young woman with horn-rimmed glasses stood blinking at him.

"Inspector Hood, how nice to see you."

"Good evening, Miss Frayle. I'm on my way back from Suffolk and thought I'd look in before going to the Yard."

He peeled off his coat and followed Miss Frayle along to the study, where Dr. Morelle moved round his desk to him and indicated a chair. The burly frame leaned back, his pipe, cold once more, jutting out from under his grizzled moustache. Crisply and incisively Dr. Morelle gave Inspector Hood a full account of the interview that had taken place that afternoon in which Ted Patrick had figured so significantly. The Scotland Yard man learned the location that had been chosen for the experiment, and the number and variety of witnesses who had duly put in an appearance. "And the only one who appeared to give you a true bill, who said straight out that nothing had happened this morning, was our friend? He claimed he was there and gave a convincing reason for his presence so early."

Dr. Morelle nodded, and the other's brow corrugated in a mystified frown. Then he gave a shrug of his thick shoulders, and prodded his pipe-bowl with a stubby finger.

"Shows integrity and observation, you might say," he said. "He was obviously telling the truth. Only it doesn't fit in with our Ted."

Inspector Hood lit his pipe, the match flaring brightly in the shadows of the study, and he pressed the burning mixture down in the bowl of his pipe and chewed at the stem for a moment. Dr. Morelle took a cigarette from the human skull which served as a cigarette-box on his desk.

"Looks as if you've had a busy day," the Scotland Yard man said, with a glance towards the mass of neatly typewritten papers on Dr. Morelle's desk. "I suppose that's all the dope on to-day's interviews?"

"That's right, Inspector," Miss Frayle said. She pushed her glasses back to the bridge of her nose. "Do you know we had over two dozen callers who reported they had seen an accident in Half Moon Street this morning, and each gave a different description of it."

For an answer, Inspector Hood drew from his inside pocket a crumpled evening newspaper. He opened it and passed it to her, so that she could see the headlines on the front page. Miss Frayle stared down at it, and then across to Dr. Morelle. She turned from the story of the robbery and the policeman's death to the Agony Column.

"I don't understand," Inspector Hood had just said to Dr. Morelle and with a nod at the newspaper. "What would be his idea?"

"I've been wondering about that," Dr. Morelle said. "And it occurred to me his statement possessed all the earmarks of a useful alibi if he should need one. That was why Miss Frayle telephoned you at Scotland Yard office, to be informed that you were in Suffolk investigating this affair." He indicated the newspaper Miss Frayle was still clutching.

"I'm pretty sure now that Ted Patrick is the chap I was trying to link with this Myra Campbell and the robbery."

"Who's Myra Campbell?" Miss Frayle inquired politely.

"Myra Campbell is Mrs. Hull's personal maid, and you might say an intimate friend of Mr. Hull."

"Oh," Miss Frayle said.

It was then that she experienced a sudden recollection of the gipsy fortune-teller at Hickham village hall. *"I see a figure, a fair figure, someone from the past,"* the dark woman had said, staring into the crystal. *"It is not a friend or acquaintance. Just someone you have seen and who is important in some way to you. And you will see this person again in the very near future."* Coming out of the tent, Miss Frayle had seen Mrs. Hull going to meet the pretty blonde young woman who had brought the sovereign. Mrs. Hull's personal maid. This was Myra Campbell. And Miss Frayle had felt convinced then that she had seen her before. Now, as Inspector Hood's words rang in her ears, she knew where it was. She shot a look at Dr. Morelle.

"It was last summer at Monte Carlo," she said.

Dr. Morelle fastened her with his hooded gaze, and took a drag at his Le Sphinx.

"What was?" Inspector Hood said.

"Where I saw her. Myra Campbell. Or rather her photographs, in all the newspapers. You remember Inspector, that Dr. Morelle and I were in Monte Carlo when he was mixed up in that odd carry-on at the Villa Midnight, and poor Dr. Morelle got shot—not fatally, I mean—that is, of course it wasn't fatal, otherwise—"

"Just explain to Inspector Hood the significance of your recollection of this young woman's photograph in the press," Dr. Morelle cut in.

"Yes, Dr. Morelle," Miss Frayle said and stopped floundering. "You see, she was in the newspapers, because she was employed at a house where there'd been a big robbery. In Nice, wasn't it? Or was it Cannes?"

"We don't know, Miss Frayle," Dr. Morelle said. "But do continue with your enthralling account."

"Well, that's all it is," she said, giving him a look. "She was mixed up in a robbery then, and now she's mixed up in this one. And that's why her face stuck in my mind."

"I don't know anything about her and this South of France business," Inspector Hood said, "but I get the drift of what you're getting at."

"I congratulate you," Dr. Morelle said.

"The trouble with all this," the other went on, leaning back in his chair, his expression heavy through a cloud of smoke from his pipe, "is that however we tie up the girl with Ted Patrick, he's got this alibi. He practically proved to you that he was in Half Moon Street at the time in question."

Dr. Morelle had been leaning casually against the corner of the writing-desk and now abruptly he turned and indicating Inspector Hood to follow him, he went through the door and into the laboratory across the hall. "There is something I'd like to show you," he said over his shoulder. As Inspector Hood followed him he turned to glance inquiringly at Miss Frayle. All she could do was give him a mystified shrug.

She hung back just inside the laboratory, which glistened with the instruments and paraphernalia everywhere, the glass doors of the shelves, the glass and steel cabinets and benches, while Dr. Morelle stood by a small movie-projector placed about the centre of the room. She had admitted a young man and the equipment to the house early that evening, and although she guessed what the equipment was, she didn't know why the young man had left it, or what manner of film it intended to show.

Dr. Morelle had remained mysteriously reticent about it. Now he drew out some chairs to place them at a suitable distance from the small screen on the wall, and as soon as Miss

Frayle and the detective had sat down, he went across and switched off the lights. He came back to the projector behind Inspector Hood and Miss Frayle, and began to run the film.

Soon there was an exclamation from Miss Frayle. But what ever was on the tip of her tongue, it remained unsaid as Dr. Morelle spoke.

"It occurred to me," he said suavely as the film continued, "that if we were intended to show how valueless was the evidence of the witnesses we would ourselves require some sort of proof. Accordingly I made arrangements for this film to be taken from the hidden vantage-point of a car. What you are now seeing is the result. An experiment similar to this," he went on, "having been carried out abroad—"

"That's right, in Paris," Miss Frayle put in.

"Yes, I know," Inspector Hood said.

"It is possible Patrick may have known of it also," Dr. Morelle said, with an irritated glance at Miss Frayle in the semi-darkness, "in which case, when he saw the advertisement, he could have deduced that it referred to something of the same nature. His need for an alibi may have been so pressing that he risked offering himself as a witness."

"The time fits in conveniently with the robbery," Inspector Hood muttered.

The film ran through. Miss Frayle got up from her chair and switched the lights on again. Inspector Hood had turned and was staring up at Dr. Morelle, his teeth clamped over his pipe, which was cold once more.

"Perhaps you'd phone the Yard and say I want a car to pick me up here," he said to Miss Frayle, without looking at her. "And tell them the quicker the sooner."

Thirty

And now Inspector Hood was shoving his gloved thumb hard against the bell-push with another impatient jab.

The mews was quiet and in darkness apart from a lighted window at the end. The parking lights of the police-car glimmered faintly on the wet cobbles, and an electric lamp burned behind the curtained windows of the flat, but no sound issued from within.

The man from Scotland Yard had left the plain clothes detective-sergeant who arrived with the car to pick him up at Harley Street sitting in his seat watching him intently. Inspector Hood had first of all wanted a little chat with Ted Patrick alone. He grunted irritably, and was about to press the bell again when he heard footsteps. The next moment the door opened and a not unfamiliar figure stood in the doorway.

For a moment Ted Patrick appeared to be scowling with surprise. He peered out at the car, then stared at Inspector Hood in a dazed fashion as if his identity was completely unknown to him. Then he recovered, and a broad smile spread across his face.

"Mr. Hood," he said, with an ostentatious display of pleasure. "I hardly recognized you. It's quite a time since we last met."

The other's heavy, square features relaxed a trifle as if he were trying to show he returned the welcome.

"It isn't, you know," he said pleasantly. "I was hoping it would be much longer."

"Always pleased to see an old friend." Ted Patrick's face looked a little pale perhaps in the light over the stairs, but his grin was confident. "What can I do for you?"

"I think you may be able to help in some inquiries I'm making," the reply came casually. "One or two little points you might be able to put me wise about."

"Certainly." The door opened wider. "Come on up and have a drink."

Inspector Hood followed him up into the living-room, his eyes narrowed a little and alert beneath his craggy brows, taking in the room. It was a plain and comfortable enough little place. He remembered that the other didn't go in for flashy display. He wasn't big-time, never had been, and he never pretended to live up to the king of underworld picture.

"Sit down, Inspector,"

The detective lowered his bulk into a chair. "I hope I won't have to stay long."

Patrick grinned at him from the sideboard, where the glasses and a bottle of whisky and gin glinted, but for all his show of confidence the detective sensed some anxiety in the man's attitude. The colour had returned to his face, or it may have been due to a trick of the light.

"Drink?"

"This isn't a social call," Inspector Hood said, with a shake of his head. "Let's get down to basics, shall we?"

Patrick held a drink for himself and he moved to the table, against which he leaned with a good attempt at an air of nonchalance.

"I'm curious," he said, and he gulped at his drink.

Inspector Hood's glance moved to the evening paper that lay on the seat of a chair. Slowly he brought his gaze until it rested again on Patrick. He jabbed his pipe-stem in the direction of the newspaper.

"Expect you've read the news?"

"I like to know what's going on." The man by the table put down his drink and calmly lit a cigarette. His eyes wandered over the headlines and back to the detective again. "I see it's your pigeon," he said.

"Been down in Suffolk best part of the day. Very professional job it turned out to be. Well-planned and all that. You know."

"Should I?" Ted Patrick smiled at him over the rim of his glass.

"Somebody from London with a local accomplice," Inspector Hood said, as if he hadn't been interrupted. "Usual routine. Stolen car from the London suburbs. House raided in the early hours after the owner had left to go over to his race-horses at Newmarket. Only the wife in the house, and she was a heavy sleeper."

"What, no servants?"

"There is one who lives in, the wife's personal maid. She was with the husband. He's that sort of husband, if you follow my meaning." The detective paused, his face grave as his eyes searched Patrick's face. "Only unusual feature about it was the killing of the police-officer," Inspector Hood said.

Ted Patrick gave a grimace.

"Rough stuff," he muttered. "That's nasty. Can't understand it. Never liked it, myself, as you know." His eyes strayed to the newspaper again. "I thought it said the copper was run down, poor chap."

"It was murder. He had instructions to stop all cars. It's obvious he tried to stop this one, driven by whoever did the breaking and entry, and he deliberately ran him down."

"Whoever he was, Inspector, he must have been out of his mind."

"Know a girl by the name of Myra Campbell?"

The sudden question caused Patrick to blink. Then he carefully considered the tip of his cigarette, and then shook his head. "Myra Campbell? Can't say I do. Blonde, brunette, or redhead?"

Inspector Hood didn't answer; his eyes were wandering round the cramped flat. "She's Mrs. Hull's personal maid," he said.

"Never heard of her, anyway," Patrick said. "The villains make a nice haul?"

"Somewhere in the region of forty thousand pounds."

Ted Patrick whistled quietly through his teeth. He took another gulp from his glass. He looked sympathetically at the stolid figure in the chair. "Wish I could help, but I've never known anyone as ambitious as that. What about the car? If it ran down the copper, there should be marks on it."

"We're looking. We think it was ditched somewhere in the vicinity. It'll be found." He sounded confident enough.

"I hope it gives you a lead," Patrick said quietly. "When you find it." And then with a wistful smile: "And so save innocent people who happen to be unlucky enough to have their names on your books having their pants scared off them."

"It's a duty we don't enjoy."

The other looked sceptical as he crushed his cigarette into an ashtray and drew a packet from his pocket. He offered it to his visitor, who gave a curt shake of his head, indicating his pipe. Patrick lit up and let a thin stream of smoke issue slowly from one corner of his mouth.

"Where were you last night and early this morning, and what were you doing?"

Inspector Hood framed the question pleasantly, but his eyes had narrowed.

"I was here last night," Ted Patrick said coolly. "Had a friend round. Harry Price. A fellow-actor. You know I've been in the profession, off and on. Mostly off, you might say, but that's the way the luck runs."

The Scotland Yard man didn't say anything, and the other went on without a tremor in his voice, or the bat of an eyelash. "Harry looked in to commiserate. We had a few drinks to-gether."

"Go on."

The thick figure in the chair began patting his pockets for matches, and found a box with which he proceeded to light his pipe, never taking his level narrowed gaze off Ted Patrick all the time. The black, charred pipe-bowl gurgled and spluttered as he drew at it.

"He left me feeling still pretty worried about things," the other went on. "Couldn't sleep. I didn't take much drink but it was enough to get me off last night for two or three hours. But I awoke at four-thirty this morning with a terrible head. I just felt I had to get out for some air. I went for a bit of a stroll, sort of aimlessly. Found myself cutting through from Oxford Street to Piccadilly. Then I sort of drifted around and got back here around sixish."

He paused and took a long drag at the cigarette.

"Only of course you can't find anyone who can corroborate that?"

Inspector Hood's expression remained grave.

Ted Patrick grinned at him. "Matter of fact I can," he said.

"I'm still interested," the detective said, and pretended to look suitably surprised.

"A certain Dr. Morelle," the other said. "Pal of yours, isn't he?" And he launched himself easily into his carefully-prepared story. "When I saw this ad I couldn't help feeling curious. I couldn't understand it. So I went along as I thought I could help. And perhaps there might have been a quid or two in it for me. There wasn't. Anyway, I thought there'd been some mistake, that they'd been misinformed. Because, of course, I was there at that time, and there'd been no accident. Nothing at all as far as I could see."

"Very strange." Inspector Hood took out his pipe from between his teeth and massaged his heavy chin.

Ted Patrick was looking at him curiously.

"What's so strange about a simple thing like that?"

The detective returned his stare. "As you say," he said, "Dr. Morelle's a bit of a pal of mine. I've just left him." He paused, his eyes watching Patrick intently. "He shot some film of Half Moon Street this morning. He ran it through for me just now. The film showed all of the street right into Piccadilly. There wasn't a soul around at the time you say you were there. You just weren't, Patrick."

Ted Patrick stood motionless, unable to speak, and then as he was about to move forward, and in the deathly silence, there came a faint metallic click and the sound of something falling to the floor. Hood's eyes fastened on the door connecting the living-room with the kitchen. A couple of strides and he had reached it and flung it open. He snapped on the light switch.

A cupboard gaped wide across the kitchen at him. On the floor sprawled a girl, her blonde hair bright in the harsh light. What had happened, he saw, was that the pressure of her body against the door had forced the snap-fastener from its socket.

Before he stooped to examine the crumpled figure he knew the girl was dead, and it took no more than a moment to recognize her. He moved to the doorway to the sitting-room. "So you never heard of Myra Campbell?"

Ted Patrick couldn't answer. He stood there, rocking slightly on his feet, his face a greyish pallor, as if the blood would never return to it, his eyes dazed.

"All right," Inspector Hood said. "There's a police-car outside. You'd better come quietly."

THE END

1696735R00081

Printed in Germany
by Amazon Distribution
GmbH, Leipzig